ISRAEL STRIKES

WILLIAM STROOCK

INTRODUCTION

This novel was first conceived in a magazine article I wrote about a fictional future Israeli attack on Iran. *Israel Strikes* is about that attack and the ensuing war. The catalyst for that war is Iran's nuclear program. As this book goes to print, that program is active and Israel has taken no overt steps to stop it. I strongly suspect that within, say, 18 months of publication, the war I describe in these pages will happen for real. This book does not try to predict that war or its course. I have no special information or contacts within any government. All the ideas contained therein are my own.

I do speculate about what that war will be like. That speculation is informed by a decade spent studying the Arab /Israeli Wars and the three Israeli conflicts with terrorists in the 2000s. I've also designed for Decision Games a war game on the topic, *Lebanon '82: Operation Peace for Galilee*. Anyone who is familiar with Israel's fight for survival will get whiffs of that past reading *Israel Strikes*; Operation Yonothan, Operation Defensive Shield, the Raid on Osirak...

On a technical note, most of the American made equipment have designations unique to the Israeli Defense Force. To avoid confusion I have used American terminology.

Lastly, thanks again to my army of editors, Kathy Yearick, Kirsten Anderson Robbins, Lee and Sharon Moyer.

William Stroock
Great Barrington Massachusetts

William Stroock

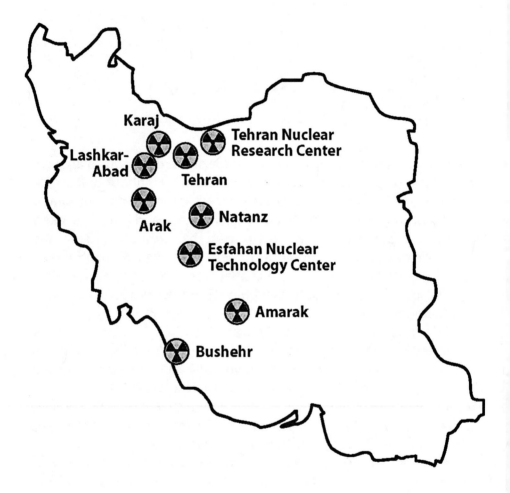

IRAN AND ITS NUCLEAR SITES
MAPS BY RENEE SULLIVAN, BURNT MILLS GALLERY

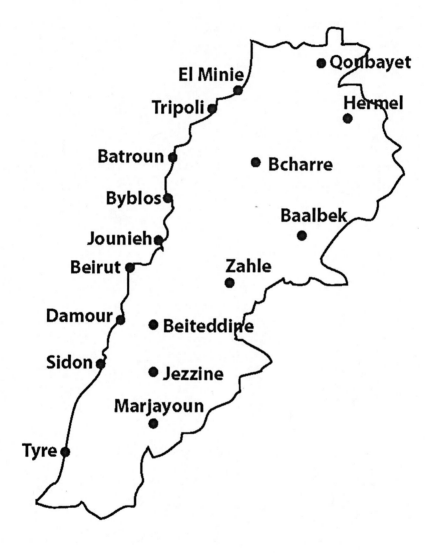

LEBANON
MAPS BY RENEE SULLIVAN, BURNT MILLS GALLERY

PART I
THE SKIES OF IRAN

CHAPTER I

BLUE STARS OVER PERSIA

As midterm elections loom, President Stettler can be thankful that there has been little controversy in the field of foreign affairs. Indeed, the Middle East has been almost serene, at least by Middle Eastern standards. In Syria, the Interim Revolutionary Council has maintained order since the expulsion of Assad. In Egypt the Muslim Brotherhood has been too concerned with domestic issues to make trouble for Israel. While the Israel-Palestinian Peace Process seems permanently frozen, the three sides, (Israel, Hamas and Fatah) are at least not shooting at one another. The only outstanding issue is the Iranian nuclear program, which experts feel is mere months away from being able to produce a nuclear weapon.

The Wall Street Journal

President With Little Foreign Policy Experience Facing Few Tests

The Washington Post

The night of the midterm elections was without a doubt the worst of my professional career; let me tell you folks, that's saying something.

Politics is partly to blame, the party in power will almost always suffer in the mid-terms. But most of the blame falls to me, my staff, and yes, the president. The president had been elected by a solid 6 point margin on a respectable record as a governor. But we tried to do too much too fast. I thought, and the president agreed, that we could move two pieces of signature legislation at once. The first of these was the president's Infrastructure Bill, our plan to revitalize the nation's roads, bridges and tunnels. The plan for a new Hudson River crossing into NYC was particularly controversial. This bill managed to unite the fiscal conservatives of both parties as well as the environmentalists against us. What was worse, we made the cardinal mistake of thinking we could push congress to do what we wanted. By that summer we had made enemies of both the House and Senate leadership.

Election night would be bad, we knew, but we didn't understand the magnitude of the defeat we were about to suffer. Nor did we know what else would happen that night.

Crisis and Victory, Gary Franks, White House Chief of Staff

What was supposed to be a night of significant but endurable losses for the party in power had turned into a disaster. The rout began on the East Coast where several incumbent congresspersons were defeated. The contagion spread to the volatile Midwest. Losses amounted to two dozen house members and four senators. The carnage was especially severe in Ohio, where the president's attorney general had run for governor and been trounced, taking with him all of the down ticket candidates for statewide office. The Mountain West was next, where the president watched his brother-in-law go down in defeat for the open senate seat in Colorado. In New Mexico the party was shattered, a particularly worrying sign for the President's reelection campaign in that crucial swing-state. Even party strongholds in Florida and Missouri had suffered losses. The coup d'état came at just after 11 PM, when the AP announced that the senate majority leader had lost his race in a squeaker to a previously unknown state senator.

At that point, President Scot Stettler had stopped watching the returns and retired to his private study just off the Oval Office. This small office was Stettler's refuge. He had decorated the room with family photos, mementos from his home state -- ice hockey trophies, pictures from hunting trips and the like, university banners and gifts from world leaders. His most cherished possession there was a bust of the great British prime minister, Robert Peel, given to him by the former British PM, and personal friend, who himself had gone down in defeat six weeks before.

Stettler drank a large whiskey, smoked cigarettes borrowed from his chief of staff, and listened to Mendelssohn's *Oveture de Hebdrides*. When Mendelsohn was finished, Stettler got up and put a new CD in the player; Tchaikovsky's *Marche Slave*. His daughter had gotten him an IPod for his birthday, but Stettler, a confirmed luddite, had not gotten around to learning how to use it. Who had the time? He sat down behind the desk and lit another cigarette, not caring for the moment if his wife found out. *She doesn't have the stresses I have*, he thought.

There was a knock on the door. 'God dammit,' he mumbled.

The door opened a crack, Gary Franks, his chief of staff said, 'Mr. President?'

'I don't need to know how badly we're doing on the West Coast, Gary.'

Franks maneuvered his considerable round and pudgy frame through the door and stepped into the office. 'Mr. President, the National Security Advisor is on the phone.'

Irritated now, the president asked, 'Yeah, what does that son-of-a-bitch want?'

'He doesn't want to discuss it on the phone, and says he needs to see you. He would like a meeting within the hour.'

'Does he?'

'He says it's important.'

'What the hell could be more important than this? With the election results in, does he want to resign?'

'I spoke to him personally, Mr. President. I don't think he would be disturbing you at a time like this unless he thought he had to. He didn't indicate to me one way or another what he wanted.'

'Sure.'

Stettler rubbed his head which was throbbing with a dull, persistent headache that two Aspirin had already failed to get rid of.

'Twelve thirty, Mr. President.'

Stettler sighed. 'Alright.'

Franks paused for a moment and said, 'I wouldn't be doing my job, sir, if I didn't tell you we are taking heavy losses on the West Coast.'

'Washington State?'

'All but gone, sir.'

Stettler didn't say anything.

'I'll leave you.'

Franks closed the door.

The National Security Advisor arrived early. The lanky, be-speckled academic, immaculately dressed in a three-piece suit as he always was, sat down in one of three chairs in front of the desk. He shifted uncomfortably in the small, minimalist chair, kept in the office by Stettler to discourage people from trying to bother him there.

'What can I help you with at *this hour*, Mr. Boddicker?'

'Mr. President, we have reason to believe that at this moment, Israel is attacking Iran.'

LAVAN ISLAND

The bored air traffic controller at Lavan Island airport looked out upon the waters of the Persian Gulf. In the distance, perhaps a mile off shore, he could see a cargo ship effortlessly floating past. Out of curiosity he picked up the tower's set of binoculars and trained it on the ship. It was a dark hulk set against the night sky, save for a pair of blinking lights at the fore and aft and one flood light on its mast, which showed the flag of Oman. He liked the idea of being out on that ship, dozing as the waves rocked him back and forth rather than being cooped up in the small, stuffy control tower. Only two other men were there with him, the radio operator, who was asleep, and a radar tech, who read passages from the Koran

6

as dozens of blips, none of them destined for Lavan, ran across his screen.

The controller stood up from his desk and said he was going outside to get some air. The two other men in the tower grunted. He walked down the stairs of the tower and outside into the cool night. About five miles to the west, the Iranian air force missile base shone in the darkness. He never understood why the government insisted on maintaining surface to air missile batteries on Lavan Island. Who would attack it?

'Sir!?' shouted the bored radioman from above. 'We have an urgent message!'

'Really?'

'Yes, sir. Incoming aircraft in trouble.'

The controller trotted inside and up the stairs. He took the radio headphones and said in English, 'This is Lavan Control Tower. What is your emergency?'

'This is Kuwaiti Air Flight Three Two Two declaring an emergency and requesting permission to land.'

'What is your emergency Flight Three Two Two?'

'Lavan Tower, we have an electrical failure and one of our engines is out.'

'Copy, Flight Three Two Two, you have permission to land.'

'I have them on the radar, sir,' said the radar tech. 'He highlighted a blue blip heading straight for Lavan from the south.

The air traffic controller gave the pilot directions, telling him to sweep over the north end of the island and come in from the west. The controller picked up the phone and rousted the airport emergency personnel from bed and ordered them to stand-to.

The plane landed three minutes later. The controller heard the engines, propeller to his surprise, but didn't see the plane because the runway lights suddenly went out, as did the lights in the control tower. To the controller's consternation the tower radar and radio were out too. He looked west to the missile base to see if the problem was localized to the airport or if the island's power plant had gone down. The missile base was dark as well.

'This is a hell of a time for a blackout,' said the controller.

He could make out the aircraft's silhouette now, it didn't conform to a typical civilian jet liner. An Iranian air force vet himself, the controller knew a military aircraft when he saw one. 'That is an American C-130,' he said.

'What?'

Before he could repeat himself, the controller saw the offloading ramp of the C-130 open. A second later a vehicle rolled down the ramp to the tarmac followed by another and still another. Men were filing out as well.

'I don't like this,' he said.

The controller picked up the tower phone but got no signal.

'I'll have to run down to the power plant,' he said.

The air traffic controller ran down the stairs and out the door toward his car. Before he got three feet, he was hit in the stomach and slammed to the ground. He felt a boot on his chest. Before he really understood what was happening, someone fell on him, slapped him in the face, affixed a thick piece of tape over his mouth, and bound his hands. Now he heard more airplane engines and the sound of helicopter rotors coming from the south, from the direction of the Omani freighter he'd seen earlier.

The controller was rolled onto his stomach. On the tarmac he could see the alleged Kuwaiti airplane. On its tail was not the Kuwaiti flag, but the Star of David.

WASHINGTON D.C.

'What do you mean,' asked the president, 'Israel is attacking Iran?'

'It is the opinion of the NSA that Israel has launched an attack on Iran.'

'What kind of attack?'

'Aerial, so far as we know.'

Stettler collected his thoughts and said, 'You mean to tell me, Israel has flown planes hundreds of miles---'

'About nine hundred, actually, sir.'

'OK, nine hundred miles across the Mideast, into Iran.'

'They're in transit. We don't think they've arrived yet.'

'What are their targets?'

'The Iranian nuclear program undoubtedly.'

Stettler leaned forward and rested his chin upon his hand. 'I suppose that makes sense.' He thought for a moment. 'Wait, how do we know this?

'Intelligence.'

'What intelligence?'

'We have human sources on the ground.'

'In Israel?'

'Yes.'

'And?'

'And they gathered information and relayed it to us.'

'Why so quiet about your sources, Mr. Boddicker?'

'I'd rather not divulge them, sir.'

'Don't trust me?'

'I trust you. It's the office of the president I don't trust.'

Stettler leaned back in his chair, looked up at the ceiling and rubbed his temples. 'Boddicker, I'm really not in the mood for this. Stop bullshitting me.'

Boddicker relented, 'Very well, Mr. President. Several intelligence sources on the ground report dozens of Israeli aircraft taking off from airbases. These include Ramat David and Tel Nof. In one case our intelligence source in Tel Nof counted 32 aircraft taking off from the base. Another 48 took off from Ramat David. There are probably more that we don't know about.'

'How long ago?'

Boddicker looked at his watch, 'Two hours and twenty two minutes ago. I received the information an hour afterwards.'

'Might this be a drill like the one they ran in the Med last year?'

'There is no unusual aerial activity in the Med.'

'So they flew over Turkey.'

'We don't know which direction they went.'

RIYADH

The personnel at the Royal Saudi Air Defence Force headquarters in Riyadh sat in silence as their radar and computer screens told them a massive wave of Israeli aircraft was violating Saudi air space- and their commander did nothing about it. Blip after blip, each representing a cluster of four Zionist jets, flew low and fast over the northern desert, northeast, toward the Arabian Gulf.

'Yes, Highness,' said the commander of the kingdom's Peace Shield air defence network. 'Yes, Highness, I understand completely. No word will be given, Highness. We shall stand down. Thank you, Your Majesty.' The commander, a timid political appointee who owed his career to the prince on the other end of the line, hung up the phone and looked around the command center, hoping none of his men could see the nervous sweat running down his forehead. He looked at the radar display showing the Zionist jets and shook his head.

On the other end of the telephone line, Prince Abdul Bin Abdullah, third in line to the throne, watched the same radar readout from his office. Only a few loyal aides were with him, as well as one of his co-conspirators, General Walid bin Rafah, Royal Saudi Army, and the prince's cousin and childhood friend.

'When did Mossad inform you, Cousin?' Rafah asked.

'An hour ago.'

'They did not leave you much time.'

'No.'

'How many aircraft do you think the Zionists will send, Cousin?' the general asked.

'Enough,' the prince responded.

'You know this?'

'I do.'

'I wish you would not keep secrets from me, Cousin.'

Prince Abdullah said nothing.

He wore his standard issue tan officer uniform with green epaulettes and red lapels. His chest bore several campaign ribbons, including one for Operation Desert Storm, where he commanded a tank company. On his desk was a picture of himself with the great

American commander, General Norman Schwarzkopf, not a keepsake but a reminder of his shame at the nation's poor performance during the war. In contrast, General Rafah wore simple army fatigues and a sidearm. Both would be needed in a few days.

WASHINGTON DC

'Can they pull it off?' Stettler asked.

'In my opinion, sir, the Israelis are capable of launching a limited one-time strike on Iran's nuclear facilities. Maybe that will hurt them, maybe it won't. I feel, and I think the secretary of Defense would agree with me, that the problem the Israelis face is that they can't follow up their attack.'

'Why not?'

'Their effort depends on speed and surprise, Mr. President. Once they hit the Iranians, the Israelis have to return to bases that are 900 miles away. If the Israelis launch a second strike, the Iranians will be waiting for them.'

'But the Israelis have a technological edge.'

'They do, Mr. President. But if they lose only a few aircraft, and God forbid the pilots are captured alive, it's a tremendous propaganda victory for the Iranians and a tremendous blow to Israel. Remember the kidnapping of Gilad Shalit?'

'So they strike Iran's nuclear programs. Which sites?'

Boddicker reached into his briefcase and took out several file folders. 'We have these prepared for you, Mr. President. They detail the targets that the NSA feels the Israelis must absolutely destroy, or at least severely damage, in order for the strike to be effective. These are the uranium enrichment facilities at Natanz and Qom, the research facility at Esfahan, the plutonium reactor at Arak, and the nuclear reactor at Bushehr, on the Persian Gulf.'

Stettler turned the pages of each folder. They showed detailed photographs, specs, and assumptions about the facilities. 'So the Israelis hit these targets and then they go home.'

'That is what we believe, yes, sir.'

LAVAN ISLAND

General Benny Peled stepped off the ramp of the C-130 knowing that for the next 72 hours he would eat, breath, sleep and make war on enemy soil. He wore simple olive army fatigues, combat boots, and a beret. Behind him, the C-130's cargo bay, packed with computers and personnel, was abuzz with action as the technicians tracked the progress of the operation.

Another C-130 was parked on the tarmac and a third was taxiing down the runway. In the distance he heard the beat of rotors as Israeli helicopters dropped Sayareet Makhal commandos on the Iranian missile base near the center of the island. Another helicopter dropped commandos on the small port on the island's south shore. Still another landed men at the oil terminal.

The first wave of Israeli F-15s was approaching the Gulf.

Peled's operations officer walked down the ramp and handed him a cup of tea. Peled took it. 'Thank you, Colonel Avi,' he said.

'General, all targets on Lavan Island are secured.'

'Casualties?'

'One Sayareet commando was wounded when an Iranian missile technician hit him in the head with a cricket bat.'

'Iranian casualties?'

'No dead, several wounded though.'

Peled looked out onto the gulf and saw the silhouette of the cargo ship growing larger.

Colonel Avi called the ship by its code name. 'Oman is being guided to the jetty. Crews remain ready to begin offloading missiles.'

'Get them started.' Peled sipped his tea. 'What about the air strip's aviation fuel tanks?'

'Near capacity.'

'Good. Call off the tankers. That's more than enough for multiple strikes.'

CHAPTER II

MACCABEE'S FIRST

During the selection process, my staff and I spent three months going through personnel folders. We wanted combat veterans, of course, but also men who had proven themselves in other fields. Several of our pilots had completed NASA's astronaut training program. Many were entrepreneurs.

A few had written and published works on history. I also wanted Maccabee Force to reflect Israel. Pilots hailed from every section of the country and every group. There were eight Christians, three Druze and two Muslim pilots in Maccabee Force.

We spent six months drilling for the attack on Iran. Daily our pilots flew out into the Mediterranean to simulate the flight to Iran. The Greek government, which has an increasingly cordial economic relationship with Israel, was helpful in this endeavor and allowed us to conduct dry runs on targets on Crete. We also conducted hundreds of live fire exercises on ranges in the Negev. I was not satisfied until each and every pilot could complete several such exercises without a single miss. Our helicopter crews and commando teams spent weeks rehearsing the seizure of Lavan Island and also rescue operations should one of our pilots be shot down.

Throughout this period, frankly, I doubted we would ever be given the order to go. As D-Day approached every time the phone rang I thought it was the chief of staff telling me to shut down operations. Deep down I never really believed we would attack.

And then we did.

Three Missions, General Benny Peled

JERUSALEM

The Israeli cabinet room was solemn. At the far end of the table, next to the doorway, sat the minister of defence with the three other cabinet members of his party. In the center on either end of the table were the ministers from the two other major parties brought into the coalition. The leader of one, the acerbic Minister for Diaspora Affairs, passed around pictures of his grandchildren living in Philadelphia. Across from him the minister of finance, Danni Shoal, talked local electoral politics with his Labour members.

At the head of the table, even though several ministers from her party were in the room, Prime Minister Yael Eitan sat alone and waited. She tried not to watch the clock affixed over the door. It mocked her, emitting a loud clicking sound with each passing minute. Eitan tried to think of other things. Her thoughts strayed to her parents, long dead now, activists and soldiers in the old Irgun and disciples of the disgraced Menachim Begin. She wondered if she had sent her career on the same trajectory as Begin's. It was not Iran she feared, at least not yet. Instead she wondered about Saudi Arabia. *Are they really going to let us overfly their territory?* She wondered. *Would Prince Abdullah really follow through on his plan?*

Mercifully the phone in front of her rang. The prime minister picked it up. 'Yes, General Ben Zvi.'

'Prime Minister,' replied the chief of staff, 'Phase One of Operation Gideon is completed and successful.'

The prime minister replaced the receiver and stood up. 'Ladies and Gentlemen, we have taken Lavan Island.'

There were sighs of relief in the room.

'As Prime Minister, I am ordering a national alert.' She turned to Shulim Levi, head of the Likud Party and minister of defence, 'Alert the army and the reserves.'

The defence minister stood. 'If you will excuse me, Prime Minister.'

She nodded. 'Of course.'

Levi Left. She looked to the ever-skeptical Danni Shoal, who returned her look and nodded his affirmation. She nodded back.

How long will I have his support, she wondered.

She turned to Yuri Alon, minister of foreign affairs and a longtime political ally. 'Mr. Alon, would you please telephone the American embassy and ask the ambassador to see me within the hour?'

LAVAN ISLAND

'General Peled. All missiles and bombs have been offloaded from Oman and are under tarps. Prisoners are being transferred to Oman as we speak.'

'Very well,' Peled said.

He stood before a large flat screen computer monitor and watched as waves of blue dots approached the four highlighted targets in Iran. The dots represented Maccabee Force, the aerial component of Operation Gideon. On this night, Maccabee Force's targets included the uranium enrichment facilities at Natanz and Qom, the research facility at Esfehan, and the plutonium reactor at Arak.

Coming up behind the attack groups were three unmanned aircraft, each the size of a small airliner, packed with electronic warfare equipment. Colonel Avi turned to his cyber warfare commander, nodded, and said, 'Now, Major Gluck.'

'Yes, General.'

The Major, who had studied at the Technion and worked IT in American and India, stood before three banks of computers, each manned by a technical sergeant piloting one of the three unmanned drones. 'Arm weapons,' the Major said.

Each man reported their electronic weapons were armed and ready.

'Activate.'

With one keystroke apiece, the technical sergeants began the largest cyber-attack in the history of warfare. False signals flooded Iranian airspace, attacking the nation's landline phones. Another signal attacked Iran's commercial and military radar net, mimicking their systems and sending false information to their radar technicians. A third signal began the complex process of attacking Iran's electrical grid. Yet another signal attacked Iran's water and sewage system.

'General, may I ask you something?'

Peled looked over his shoulder. He had completely forgotten that he was accompanied by a young reporter who introduced himself to Peled as a 'gonzo' journalist. He looked at the reporter and then turned his attention back to the flat screen monitor.

'Yes, Gonzo,' he said.

'General, why attack Iran's water and sewage network? What military significance do they have?'

'By attacking civil infrastructure, we are creating a crisis of and in the government. No water, no power. The more problems the Iranians have to deal with, the better.'

The reporter waited for Peled to say more. The general ignored him. Instead he walked over to the bank of cyber-warfare computers and watched as data poured across their computer screens.

'General,' said Colonel Avi, 'Strike Group Simon is approaching Natanz.'

Peled walked back to the main computer readout. It showed a photo of Natanz taken by a drone. A picture box in the corner showed the site's three underground centrifuge bunkers. Peled touched the screen bringing up a blue box describing Strike Group Simon's components: Twelve F-15s armed with eight GUB-39 bunker busters, each capable of penetrating up to three feet of concrete. Behind the Eagles were 10 F-16 Falcons armed with a pair of one ton smart bombs.

'General, Strike Group Simon signals all clear and proceeding.'

'Very well. Put them on speaker,' ordered Peled.

There was no sound as Strike Group Simon maintained radio silence until the last possible moment. Finally. 'This is Simon-Aleph,' said the strike group leader, 'I am making my attack run.'

Simon-Aleph accelerated and approached the first bunker. 'Approaching Target-One, aiming….' There was a beeping sound. 'Target-One painted…bombs away.' All in the command center could hear the roar of Simon-Aleph's engines as he banked and accelerated away from the facility.

'…target hit! Target hit!' reported Simon-Bet. 'This is Simon-Bet approaching Target-One…target painted,' more beeping, '…bombs away…' again the sound of accelerating jet engines. 'Hit! Hit! Multiple blasts.'

'This is Simon-Vet. Approaching Target-One…Target painted… bombs away…'

'Oh my god, look at that explosion!' someone said.

'Shut-up Simon-Dalet and begin your attack on Target-Two.'

'Yes, Simon-Aleph.'

One by one the other F-15s attacked Target-Two, and then Target-Three.

When the F-15s were finished the F-16s launched their attack on Natanz. Their targets were the above ground administrative and research buildings throughout the site. Each was set alight by the attacking F-16s, who each dropped two GBU-27 laser guided bombs through the roofs, crashing through several floors before exploding. When they were finished, Simon-Aleph signaled. 'Well done… returning.'

In fact, Strike Group Simon would be returning nowhere and instead flying to a new location entirely.

'It looks like you've smashed Natanz,' said Gonzo.

Peled only responded, 'We shall see.'

Minutes later the scene at Natanz was repeated at the nuclear enrichment facility at Qom. Strike Group Judas' Six F15s unleashed 42 GBU-39s from their standoff positions to the south. Thirty six of these were targeted on Qom's underground centrifuge bunker while the remaining six hit the two adjacent power plants. As at Natanz a dozen

F-16s followed up the strike with 20 GBU-27 laser guided bombs targeted on the centrifuge bunker.

Peled listened in as, to his annoyance, the pilots couldn't seem to shut up.

'Huge explosions!' said one.

'I see them, look at that place burn!'

Peled waited for the next action, Strike Group Eleazar at Arak. As it was built above ground, the plutonium reactor did not require bunker busters; as such no F-15s were part of Strike Group Eleazar. Instead the attack was carried out by one dozen F-16s. Like the previous two strikes, Eleazar encountered no ground fire at the target. The first wave attacked Arak's containment dome, cooling tower, and exhaust stack. Each was struck by two F-16s apiece. The remaining six F-16s struck Arak's heavy water plant, storage facility, cooling towers, and distillation and exchange plant.

Each pilot, dispassionately reported, 'Engaging...bombs away... target hit...'

'Heavy water plant?' Gonzo asked.

'Yes,' replied Peled.

'Aren't you concerned about environmental damage?'

Peled looked at Gonzo. 'You might want to the consider the environmental damage to Tel Aviv if it is destroyed in a nuclear attack.'

Gonzo conceded Peled's point with a shrug and a nod.

Strike Force Jonathon attacked next. Their target was the uranium conversion facility outside Esfahan. Six F-15s and 10 F-16s swooped down on the base, targeting the fuel manufacturing facility and the conversion facility. Each of these buildings received four GBU-27s. Once the F16s had departed the remaining six F-15s attacked the tunnel complex, built into a mountain just northeast of the main facility. Rather than trying to penetrate the mountain, the pilots delivered bunker busters to both tunnel entrances in the hopes of forcing a catastrophic collapse.

As reports flooded in over the radio, Colonel Avi said, 'It looks like we hit the tunnel entrances. That was toughest target.'

Peled watched the flat screen monitor. It showed blue dots moving south, except for a half dozen, single F-16s racing west, and accelerating to supersonic speed over Iranian cities.

'Why send six jets back to Israel?' asked Gonzo.

'Those pilots will make much noise. Their sonic booms will draw attention, break windows. They will help the Iranians think every aircraft is returning to Israel.'

The reporter hurriedly scribbled notes.

'How would you say the attack is going?' Gonzo asked.

'Too soon to tell.'

As dawn approached the strike groups began to land at Lavan. Strike Group Simon was first. Each aircraft was quickly taxied under a camouflage tarp. The airport's lone fuel truck pulled up alongside the jets and began refueling.

'Isn't that going to be slow?' asked Gonzo.

'Yes, but I don't want to risk refueling them at the tanks. They could be spotted in the open.'

Nearby ground crewmen loaded bombs onto pushcarts and prepared to take them over to the assembled jets. Many of the pilots took drinks and snacks. The pilots greeted each other and shook hands. Before they could trade notes though, Colonel Avi ordered them into the control tower where they would be debriefed. As an amused Peled looked on, one jumped from the cockpit and demanded to know where the nearest bathroom was. At the far end of the runway, the first of four unmanned drones took off.

As Strike Group Judah came in, and Strike Group Eleazar approached, Peled went back to his command center. Colonel Avi reported, 'Iranian power and communication still down. We're picking up a lot of military and civilian radio chatter.'

'What do they say?'

'They know they're under attack. They're not sure of the magnitude and are getting dozens of false reports.'

'I guess the flares we dropped on the way out did their job.'

'I suspect, sir.'

'So the Iranians are completely confused.'

'Yes, sir. I would say that right now, they don't know what they don't know.'

'Good.'

'General?' asked Gonzo. 'May I go interview your pilots, now that they've been debriefed?'

Peled looked at Avi, and nodded.

'Thank you.'

Gonzo hurriedly walked out of the command center like a child being told by his mother not to run.

'One other report, General.'

'Yes?'

'Western media has gone live and is reporting our attack.'

WASHINGTON DC

President Stettler returned to the Oval Office while he waited for his cabinet to assemble in the Situation Room. Boddicker was already down there. The secretary of State and the secretary of defense were on the way. Ominously, word had come from Jerusalem that Ambassador Silber had been summoned to meet with Prime Minister Eitan. Stettler reached into his pocket and took out a bottle of Aspirin. He'd been keeping one there for the last month to fight the now nearly constant headaches, and took another two. *God I did not want to have to deal with the Middle East in my term*, he thought. *Is there any president who came out of the region looking good?* He thought of Carter, Reagan, Clinton, the Bushes, Obama…

Franks entered the Oval Office and switched on the TV in the corner. He fumbled with the remote control until he found the BBC.

'Goddamn it, Franks, I don't want any more election updates.'

"I'm not giving you any, sir. Here is what's on the BBC."

The screen was split. On the left screen was a Middle Eastern man speaking in an impeccable English University accent. On the right was a grainy image of the Tehran skyline. It was pierced by tracer fire and occasional explosions. A female reporter described what she saw in the air and heard on the ground. '…explosion, windows rattle. Hundreds of car alarms have gone off.'

'Erica, what action, if any, has the Iranian government taken?'

'Well, Martin, my contacts within the Iranian government are not yet offering comment.'

'Have you seen any activity? Police in the streets? Troops on the move?'

'My cameraman, while I was dialing the BBC office in London, saw a small convoy of military trucks; that was perhaps 30 minutes ago. Other than that…'

Franks spoke, 'Mr. President, CNN's man in Jerusalem is reporting that air raid sirens are blaring there as well.' Franks turned the channel to CNN, which showed a reporter standing before the Jerusalem sky-line. Air raid sirens were audible in the background. 'And then there's this.'

Franks turned the channel again, this time to Fox, which was running a loop of one of their reporters in Jerusalem being ordered off the air by Israeli officials. When the reporter refused, a pair of police-men came on camera and grabbed him. The last few seconds showed an Israeli policeman swinging a baton at the camera.

'Jesus,' said Stettler.

'Well, Mr. President, if you want corroborating evidence for Boddicker's intel, I think you have it.'

'We'll just have to wait for Ambassador Silber's report.'

JERUSALEM

Prime Minister Eitan stood up as Ambassador Silber walked into her office. She came out from behind her desk and shook his hand.

'Ambassador, I do thank you for coming here on such short notice.'

Silber gave a slight bow. 'Not at all, Prime Minister.'

'I trust your trip was without issue.'

'Oh yes, Prime Minister. Though it was loud,' he said in reference to the air raid sirens.

'Please sit.'

Silber sat down in front of the desk. The prime minister returned to hers.

Her expression changed from pleasant welcome to stone-face seri-ousness. 'Ambassador Silber, it is my duty as Prime Minister to inform the United States that the State of Israel has commenced military operations against Iran.'

The ambassador was nonplussed. 'I thought so, Prime Minister.' He cleared his throat. 'Of course, I cannot, in my capacity as ambassador, say anything about the action at this time. Not until I receive instructions from my government.'

'Of course.'

'The secretary of state, and the president, would be grateful for any information on the attack you are able to provide.'

The prime minister nodded. 'And I can extend you that courtesy.' She took a folder off of her desk and handed it to Ambassador Silber. 'This folder may not leave my office. But I can allow you to read it if you like.'

Ambassador Silber took the folder and opened it. There were a dozen papers inside. Without looking up as he read, he asked. 'May I take notes?'

Eitan held out her hand. 'Please.'

Ambassador Silber took a pen and small note pad out of his interior coat pocket. The gray-haired, be-speckled lawyer licked his fingers, opened the pad, and clicked his pen. He leafed through each page, deliberately taking down a few notes with each one. When he was finished, he handed the folder back to Eitan.

'May I ask you a few questions, Prime Minister?'

'Yes. Though you realize, I cannot discuss any plans.'

He cleared his throat once more, 'Do you have contingencies for further conflict with Iran?'

'Yes.'

'Do those contingencies involve either Lebanon or Syria?'

'Yes.'

'Will you consider any offensive action against those nations, or elements within those nations?'

'We have taken no options off the table.'

'I see.' Ambassador Silber adjusted his glasses and said, 'I will, of course report this meeting to the secretary of state and the president. Is there any message you would like me to relay?'

'None at this time. But, I would be grateful for the president's council. Might he be available for a telephone conversation within the next day or two?'

'I should think so.'

'Very well then.'The prime minister stood up.'If you will excuse me, Mr. Ambassador…'

Ambassador Silber stood as well.'Of course, Prime Minister.'

As she led him to the door, the prime minister said.'Please convey to President Stettler my sympathies on the election.'

Ambassador Silber smiled wryly.'I will.'

'And I am sorry for putting this issue on his desk at this time.'

They shook hands.

Ambassador Silber left the prime minister's residence and got in the back of his limo. *Of course you're sorry*, he thought. *I bet.*

WASHINGTON D.C.

President Stettler took his seat at the head of the table. On his left was the secretary of defense, the former chair of the House Armed Services Committee. Behind his back, Stettler and Franks referred to Secretary Davis as 'More-More'- more missiles, more tanks, more jets, more, more, more. On the right was the secretary of state. Secretary Wesson had served several administrations in various roles, and looked upon the State Department, Stettler knew, as the culmination of a long career in public service. Gary Franks felt he lacked 'the balls' in his words, for the job, but Stettler liked the man for his experience.

Stettler looked at the large flat screen television at the end of the room. It showed Ambassador Silber from the embassy in Jerusalem.

'Alright Mr. Ambassador. What did the prime minister say?'

'She takes full responsibility for the attacks on Iran. The prime minister allowed me to view a dossier detailing the plan. I took extensive notes. The Israelis have launched more than one hundred aircraft at Iran.' He listed the various nuclear targets.

'I don't understand,' said the secretary of defense, 'What do they expect to achieve with a limited strike?'

'Well, that's the thing, Mr. Secretary, the strike isn't limited.'

'How so?' asked Davis.

23

'The Israelis have seized an Iranian airbase on an island in the Persian Gulf. As we speak, Israeli aircraft are landing, refueling, and rearming.'

'So this isn't a simple raid like Iraq in 1981,' said Wesson. 'They mean war.'

'Mr. Ambassador,' asked Boddicker, 'Are you in the bunker?'

'I am. The entire country is on alert. I don't know if you can hear them, but every air raid siren in the country must be blaring.'

'What did the prime minister say in the meeting?' the president asked.

'Very few specifics. She asked if it would be possible to speak with you sometime in the next few days, Mr. President.'

Stettler looked over at Franks and nodded. Franks nodded back. He looked back to the flat-screen. 'Ambassador, is there anything else? What can you tell us?'

Silber cleared his throat. 'Well, Mr. President, the prime minister is in a very sticky situation.'

'I am aware of Israel's military predicament.'

'Yes, sir, but politically she is in a very precarious position.'

'I don't think that matters right now, Ambassador,' said Stettler.

'With all due respect, sir, it does. She holds a shaky, two-seat majority coalition government with the secular parties, Kadima, Labour, and Likud of course. Arrayed against her is the Shas-Torah United Party. These are the orthodox hardliners, and they hate her. If Shas-Torah were to unite with the settler hardliners in Israeli Beiteinu, they would have a narrow majority. The President of Israel would have no choice but to ask their leaders to form a new government.'

'If I may, Mr. President,' interjected Franks, 'Israeli Beiteinu takes a hard line stance on the Palestinian Authority as well as Iran. It would be difficult for them to oppose Prime Minister Eitan if she could present herself as the woman who saved Israel from the Mullahs.'

'I agree, Mr. President,' said Silber.

'So you think she's doing this to improve her approval ratings?' Wesson asked.

'Her government is in big trouble. From a political standpoint, this strike could save her. That said, I know the prime minister pretty well. I don't think she would order this attack unless there was a military necessity to do so.'

Wesson spoke, 'Do they realize they may be starting a wider Mideast war?'

There was chatter and crosstalk as the assembled advisors speculated about what would happen next. Stettler rubbed his head in annoyance. 'What about it, Ambassador Silber? What are the Israelis planning next?'

'They won't tell me.'

'Lebanon is the next obvious step,' said Davis. 'Hezbollah is deeply rooted in the south, and has a plurality in the Lebanese cabinet.'

'That might also mean Syria,' said Boddicker.

'Will Israel attack Lebanon and Syria?' asked Stettler.

'Prime Minister Eitan said all options are on the table. Direct quote, sir,' said Silber.

'Oh, lord,' said Davis.

There was more chatter and crosstalk. Franks raised his hands. 'One thing at a time. One thing at a time.'

'Thank you,' said the president. 'OK. Ambassador Silber, do you think Israel will attack?'

'I can't say. I don't know. All I can tell you is that if they think they have to attack Lebanon, they will.'

'OK. What will the Syrians do?' asked Davis.

Wesson cleared his throat. 'The Interim Revolutionary Council has never said publically what it would do in case of an Israeli invasion of Lebanon.'

'The council is a mess right now,' said Wesson.

'Yes. So a little war with the Zionist Entity might be just what they need to tamp down descent and unify the country,' said Boddicker.

The president rubbed his head again. 'So if I understand you gentleman correctly. Israel is attacking Iran. Iran may order its proxy in Lebanon to attack Israel. Ambassador Silber, is it your opinion that Israel will invade Lebanon in such an event?'

'Yes.'

'If Israel invades Lebanon, then Syria may attack Israel.'

The assembled secretaries nodded their heads. So did Silber.

'That's just great,' said Stettler. 'Where are we? Europe in 1914?'

Franks said, 'It does look that way, Mr. President.'

Stettler rubbed his head again.

'So if Syria attacks what do the Jordanians do? What about Egypt…
or the Turks…'

LAVAN ISLAND

To simulate the normal chatter Iran would receive from Lavan, the
airport control tower was manned by half a dozen Persian Jews who
spoke Farsi at home. Supervising the operation was an Iranian Kurd
who had been working with the Israelis for decades. The SAM base's
communications had been re-routed to the tower as well, and the
man designated to impersonate the base commander had already
received word from the Iranian Air Force to go on alert. There was no
indication that the Iranian government suspected trouble on Lavan.
So far, the ruse was working.

The Israelis were winning the cyber war. Major Gluck had decided
to attack the land lines, crashing their host systems and rendering
them useless. However, they left the cell phone network intact. Many
government and military officials were chatting away in the clear,
enabling the cyber warfare team to put together a pretty clear picture
of what the Iranians knew, and what they didn't know.

Major Gluck reported the situation to the Colonel Avi and General
Peled, 'At first they thought they were under attack, then the military
insisted there wasn't an attack and the explosion at Natanz must have
been some sort of accident. I laughed when I heard one Air Force general explain that if the Zionists launched an attack, his forces would
have shot them down. The Iranian government now understands
they are being attacked. They think it's us. Their defense efforts are
being hampered by our cyber-attack. Air defense is down, radar is a
mess.'

'Good,' said Peled.

'What's more interesting is that we're seeing massive infight-
ing within the government. The Army is angry at the Air Force. The
Pasdaran is pointing fingers at the military. The Revolutionary Council
is pointing fingers at everyone.'

'Keep monitoring it.'

'Someone up there,' Avi nodded to the north, 'is keeping his head, and slowly government and military officials are shutting up. So we shall have diminishing returns.'

'What is the status of their computer network?'

'The defense ministry is being subjected to a vicious denial of service attack. Anyone visiting the MOD's various sites, Army, Air Force, etc, will receive an error message. This is also the case with various energy providers. We have left up the Ministry of Information website, though.'

'Why?'

'At the moment, we control it. I cannot say for how long, because sooner or later their own IT people will fix the problem, but right now, we control the site and are putting out false information.'

'Such as?'

'If one visits the Ministry of Information, they will see denunciations of America and claims that they have proof that the Americans, in conjunction with their British lackeys, are attacking the Islamic Republic.

'When the Iranians finally determine how we have hacked into the Ministry of Information site and block us out, we've left a little worm in their system. General, I think you will be able to appreciate the worm's irony.'

Peled nodded.

Their conversation was interrupted by the commander of the drone force. 'General Peled, Colonel Avi?' he said, 'First drone is approaching Natanz. We have it on the horizon now.'

Peled walked over to the airborne command center. Inside were a dozen drone consuls, each manned by an airman. The operation's officer led him to the consul for the Natanz drone. Before the airman was a color monitor which showed the drone's nose camera. At 10,000 feet the ground below gently rolled past. A few miles away they could see smoke plumes and a large fire. As the drone got closer they could tell that the fire came from the facilities' administrative building. The airman zoomed the camera in. The great complex, as large as some office parks, was engulfed in flames.

'What about the centrifuge bunkers?'

'Heading their now, sir,' said the airmen.

He turned his joystick to starboard. The view on the monitor slanted and then leveled off. Each centrifuge bunker was more than 300,000 square feet and fed by a single tunnel entrance. They were dozens of feet underground but identifiable by the dirt fields above them.

'Look at the north bunker. Zoom in, zoom in,' said Colonel Avi.

The airman zoomed as tight as he could, so that the bunker filled the screen.

The field above the bunker had cratered in two places, smoke billowed from each.

'Looks like we scored a direct hit,' said Avi.

'Mmmm,' Peled replied.

'Now the south bunker,' Avi ordered. 'Zoom in on the south bunker.'

The airman zoomed out and then in on the south bunker. There was only one crater there, but it was much larger than those on the north bunker. Smoke billowed there as well, and through the haze, they could see orange fire.

'What about the tunnel entrance?'

The airman zoomed out again and then in on the joint tunnel entrance. They could tell that the entrance had collapsed, so thoroughly that only thin wisps of smoke were evident despite the conflagration inside. Ambulances and fire trucks were parked nearby, but there didn't seem to be much activity.

'Not much happening down there,' said Colonel Avi. 'Maybe we got their night shift. We know they have one.'

'That is a lot of dead people,' Peled said. 'We have seen enough. Get the drone out of there before the Iranians realize what it is.'

'Yes, General.'

Slowly, over the next few hours Israeli drones arrived over the other targets. At Qom the power plants were in flames. There was no fire at the site of the underground bunker, but there was a football field length gash in the earth, indicating that the entire underground facility had collapsed in on itself. At Arak the heavy water plant, cooling towers, storage facility, and distillation plant were all piles of smoldering rubble. The research facility outside of Esfahan was engulfed in flames.

A fourth drone flew over the nuclear reactor at Bushehr. Even though Maccabee Force hadn't attacked it yet Peled was just as concerned with its status. The drone camera showed the plant, fully intact. Several armored cars and other military vehicles ringed the plant, and they could make out a cluster of mobile SAM batteries and truck mounted anti-aircraft guns. Even from 10,000 feet they could see hundreds of soldiers ringing the plant. A pair of naval ships bobbed in the waters of the Persian Gulf nearby. A half dozen helicopters were in the air. Colonel Avi was about to say something when the saw a flash on the ground followed by several others.

'They've spotted the drone,' said Avi.

'Get it out of there,' said Peled. He thought for a second and said, 'Colonel, a damage assessment within the hour. Drone intelligence, pilot debriefings, everything. I must brief the chief of staff.'

'Yes, General.'

'And get your pilots ready. I want to hit the second round of targets this afternoon.'

'Yes, sir.'

CHAPTER III

WAR FOR THE AIR

For a modern nation state the key to victory, real victory that secures a better peace, is winning the media war. One nation can obliterate the armed forces of another, but a victory reliant on battlefield success is incomplete. The world must see that that nation has achieved said victory. The world must also believe that the nation that has achieved a battlefield victory has done so under the auspices of what may be called 'just war'. The world must believe, or be made to believe, that said nation was justified in going to war. The world must also see that the war was fought 'morally'. Did the victorious nation strive to avoid civilian casualties? Did they try to avoid damage to civilian infrastructure? Did they avoid the use of weapons deemed unacceptable to the international community such as land mines, cluster munitions, and white phosphorous? A nation failing to live up to these expectations has won a military victory but lost in the political realm.

It is therefore vital that any warring nation not only be prepared to fight on the physical field of battle, but the digital field of battle as well ...

Digital Victory in Modern War,

Professor Annon Statch

JERUSALEM

Prime Minister Eitan walked into a small conference room full of officers standing at attention. She stood in front of the podium and told the officers to be seated.

'By now, you all know that the task you have trained for is at hand.' There were nods and murmurs.

'Ladies and gentlemen, I want to be clear. Your job is just as important as the one being performed by our brave pilots. You are our international vanguard. It is your duty to take to the airwaves, all airwaves, and deliver our message to the world. That message is simple. Israel is a pluralistic democracy acting in self-defense against a soon to be nuclear armed regime that has pledged our destruction. You must be candid, you must be forthright, you must take whatever verbal abuse is hurled at you with good cheer, and you must deliver the facts, no matter what.'

She paused and made eye contact with the assembled men and women. Her eyes fell first to their chief press officer, Colonel Avigdor Zev. He spoke English with a British accent and Arabic like a native of Baghdad; his parents fled Iraq in the 1950s. He would deal almost exclusively with news networks in Great Britain, as well as Canada, Australia, and other commonwealth nations. Next her eyes fell upon a pair of lieutenants, a young man and young woman. The young man played basketball in the Israeli league, while the young woman had done some modeling in Israel before becoming a helicopter pilot. Both had lived and travelled extensively in the United States. They would go on American networks like MTV and The Daily Show as a young duo to tell American kids what Israel was about. Next she came to a 40ish tank commander who had earned a scar across his face in Lebanon, and after that had served in Gaza. The rest of that face was smooth and chiseled, a shock of salt and pepper hair was atop his head. It was calculated, and the prime minister saw it herself, that he would appeal to Western women. Next came a tall, slender black woman who had been evacuated from Ethiopia in the late 90s; she would appear on television in Africa. Then she came to Major Romi Ben Joseph, an Arabic-speaking medical doctor. To him fell the difficult task, and Eitan thought, unenviable duty, of taking to the airwaves of al-Jazeera, among other Arab language networks.

'Are there any questions?' There were none. 'Very well, then. I have complete confidence in you.' She looked out at the assembled men and women once again and then motioned for them all to stand up. She walked over to the line of officers and shook each one's hand, exchanging pleasantries and small talk. She was chatting with the young duo when an aide walked into the room.

'Prime Minister, the Chief of Staff needs to see you.'

'Well ladies and gentlemen, I am needed elsewhere.'

They saluted as she left the room. Eitan was led up to her office. Waiting there was the Chief of Staff. He stood and saluted. Instead of sitting behind her desk, Eitan sat in the chair next to the Chief. General Moshe Ben Zvi was one of the generation of new officers who had been fighting modern war against non-state actors. He had commanded a tank platoon in Lebanon in 1982, but otherwise his military experience was entirely in counterterrorism. He had fought in the trio of Israeli wars in the 2000s, against Fatah in 2002, Hezbollah in 2006, and Hamas in 2009 and had absorbed the hard way the lessons of modern war, that one dead civilian could undo all the work of a successful snatch and grab operation, that the image on international news of a single burning Israeli tank did far more damage to the State of Israel than the actual loss of the tank; that the capture of a hundred terrorists could never undo the pain felt by the nation of a single captured Israeli soldier.

'Prime Minister, I have spoken with General Peled. He reports that the Natanz, Arak, and Esfahan sites have been heavily damaged. Esfahan and Arak are in flames. The bunkers at Natanz appear to have collapsed.'

'Is he sure?'

'He personally viewed the drone camera footage as it was relayed back to his headquarters. The footage is consistent with pilot reports, and the footage from their gun and smart bomb cameras.'

'What are our losses?'

'None,' he replied, 'So far.'

'What about the Iranians? What is their situation?'

'For the moment, mass confusion. But that won't last, Prime Minister.'

'They are already taking to the airwaves to denounce us.'

'I know.'

'The BBC and al-Jazera have joined them.'

'I know. In an hour I must take to the airwaves myself and tell the Israeli people what we have done on their behalf.' Eitan cleared her throat. 'Now, what does Peled plan next? Is he coming home?'

'No, he is going to begin the second phase of the operation. We expect to take casualties in this phase. The targets will be much tougher.'

'God help those pilots,' she said.

'Indeed.'

She stood up. 'Thank you, General.'

General Ben Zvi stood and saluted.

'After I address the nation, I would like, if it is not too much trouble, to come down to the operations center and listen in.'

'Of course, Prime Minister. It would be my pleasure.'

When he left, the prime minister thought, *God help* me *if we fail.*

WASHINGTON D.C.

President Stettler hadn't felt this sick since his college hockey team lost in the semi-finals. In the final game of the seven game series, he had driven on the opposition's goal and shot, only to see the puck, which he aimed for a gap between the goaltender and the goalpost, ping against the goalpost. The ping sound made by the puck echoed in his mind for weeks after, and on bad nights he often heard it in his dreams. The next morning had been the worst of Stettler's life as he dealt with the feeling failure and disappointment, fended off taunts, and worse, expressions of sympathy.

This morning felt even worse. Mrs. Stettler was already up and out with their daughter, who attended a special morning session of school before leaving in the afternoon for the set of her MTV reality show, *First Daughter*. He shook his head and blamed himself. On election night, he had concluded his victory speech by calling Kelly over, then 16, hugging her, and saying into the microphone, 'And in case you're wondering boys, she's available.' Kelly had recoiled in horror. MTV ran the clip dozens of times in the next few days and even interviewed Kelly. After the interview she was approached by producers about a reality show, which they felt, could lead to other shows down the line about Kelly's tastes. One hopeful producer even pitched a show with the working title, *Dating the First Daughter*. For his part Stettler was glad his daughter was at all times under armed escort.

As Stettler donned his black suit, blue shirt and red tie, he looked at the headlines of the morning papers on his dresser. They were concerned with the election as all had gone to print before the Israeli air strike began. *The Washington Post* was the most charitable with the big, bolded headline 'President Rebuked'. 'Presidential Wipeout', mocked *The Examiner*. Tabloids were the most creative. The *New York Post* featured a mockup of the president in court before a judge with the accompanying headline, 'Voters Issue Restraining Order'. When he finished reading these, Stettler turned the TV on, he usually liked to listen to the morning gabfests while he dressed. But as soon as he did he was confronted with a panel which debated whether or not the Israeli strike on Iran was his failure as well. He turned the TV off.

After taking a light breakfast in the residence he went downstairs to the Oval Office. Franks was already there. Though he had no doubt slept even less that Stettler, he looked fresh and relaxed in a dark blue suit, blue shirt, and blue tie. Boddicker was waiting as well.

The two men stood. 'I was about to send someone to get you, sir.'

'Where are the secretaries of defense and state?'

'They are en route now.' Franks cleared his throat. 'We have news.'

'Election, or Middle Eastern?'

'Middle Eastern. Prime Minister Eitan is due to address the Knesset.'

They turned on the TV in Oval Office and waited. Secretaries Davis and Wesson arrived just as Prime Minister Eitan was taking the podium before the Knesset.

'A lot of empty seats there,' Davis said.

'Dozens of MKs are reservists and have no doubt been called up,' Boddicker said.

Franks shushed everyone as the prime minister began to speak.

'People of Israel…'

'She's speaking in English,' said Stettler.

'She's speaking to the world,' Boddicker said.

Franks interjected, 'Shh…'

'I come to the Knesset today to announce that, as of this moment, the State of Israel is at war with the Islamic Republic of Iran…'

'War,' Wesson said. 'She says they're at war.'

'As I speak to you this afternoon, the brave men and women of the Israeli Defense Forces are destroying the tools with which the Islamic Republic of Iran has pledged our destruction. This government will not rest until those tools are removed from the hands of those who would use them.'

She went on listing the nature of the Iranian nuclear program and took considerable time to quote International Atomic Energy Commission reports on their various facilities and UN resolutions on the matter. 'I regret that the combined efforts of the international community have failed to stop the mullah's nuclear program, and I regret that the government of Israel had to take these defensive actions. But no one, least of all the Mullah's, should confuse regret with irresoluteness. Let there be no doubt,' With each word she pounded the podium. 'The government of Israel will take whatever steps are necessary - any steps necessary - to defend the Jewish State.'

For the first time the Knesset broke into applause. It was loud and roaring and took nearly a minute to subside.

'The Jewish people will no doubt suffer. But has it ever been another way? We have been struck by the hand of Pharaoh and the Romans, the Crusaders and Byzantines, the Mufti and the Nazis. But now when the hand of evil strikes the Jewish people, the Jewish people can strike back. And so we have. And so we will!'

'That's apocalyptic,' said Davis.

Her voice rose to a crescendo, 'Iran's nuclear program ends now.' There as more applause in the Knesset. It was at that point that the prime minister switched to Hebrew.

'Well, I think she got her point across,' said Boddicker.

'And what was her point?' Wesson asked.

'This is a war to the death.'

'What do you mean?'

To Stettler's eyes, Boddicker became irritated. 'This isn't some daring night raid against a small target. It's a campaign against Iran.'

Secretary Wesson was flabbergasted. 'Well, I sincerely doubt the Israelis would precipitate a wider Mideast war when we could negotiate--'

Boddicker interrupted him. 'Mr. Secretary,' he said firmly, 'you negotiators have been trying for a decade to put a stop to this, and the Israelis clearly feel you failed.'

'But the potential admittance of Israel to NATO-'

Now Boddicker got mean. 'Ha, ha. You mean the Jews are going to count on the Spanish, French, and oh yes, the Germans to protect them. To them that is a sick joke.'

Wesson was silent for a few moments. 'Well I just don't think you understand the engagement process.'

'Gentlemen…' Franks said.

Stettler watched the exchange in fascination. It was not the first clash between Boddicker and the secretary of state, but still, he'd never heard Boddicker say anything remotely like that. *What does that man want?* He asked himself. Of the three cabinet men gathered there, Davis was a career politician trying to pad his resume, Wesson was a do-gooder, only Boddicker was a real intellectual. He had been a key advisor on the campaign, and when Stettler had first met the man, in his study in Georgetown, he had found the sheer mass of history and political books to be overwhelming. After the election, Boddidcker had, to Stettler's surprise, turned down the State Department post and instead asked for the NSA. Watching Boddikcer joust with Wesson, and the almost dismissive tone he took toward the career civil servant, Stettler started to feel he finally understood why. *He thinks Wesson's job is nothing but a messenger boy's.*

Franks held up his hands. 'Alright gentlemen. I think we need to stop bickering and discuss matters with the president.'

'Agreed,' said Boddicker. Wesson remained silent.

'What do we know so far?' Stettler asked.

Boddicker spoke first. 'The Israelis have attacked Iran. This attack is not just a preemptive strike but the first blow in an all-out war.'

'Do we know what kind of damage the Israelis inflicted?' Stettler asked.

Boddicker reached into his briefcase and took out a folder. 'We have detailed satellite photographs.'

'And?'

'The Israelis really whacked them, sir,' said Boddicker.

'What does that mean?' Davis asked.

'We don't have anybody on the inside, but judging by what we've seen,' he handed the folder to Stettler, who began flipping through the pages, 'They did tremendous damage to four sites.'

Stettler looked at the photo of the Arak site and whistled in wonderment. 'Damn...'

'Indeed,' Boddicker added. 'I have a few sources in Israel,' he nodded, 'Knowledgeable, who say the Israelis are, thus far, happy with the results.'

'If they're happy, why are they continuing the attack?' Wesson asked.

'Because they have big plans,' Boddicker smirked.

LAVAN ISLAND

General Peled huddled in the corner of the command center with his staff.

He looked at Colonel Avi, 'What do we know about the targets?'

'Our sources, both electronic and human, report that they are buzzing with activity. Lots of comings and goings, lots of VIPs.'

'Mobilization?'

'The regular army no, the Pasdaran and Revolutionary Guard Corps, yes.'

'What do you think that means?'

'They may not trust the army.'

'And the navy?'

'Aside from the ships around Bushehr, still in port.'

'Good.' He turned to Major Gluck. 'What do you know?'

'We feel that the Iranian technical experts are cleaning out their system. The lights in Tehran went on a few hours ago, but their air defense network is still down. By the tone of the communications we are able to monitor, the Iranians are still in a panic.'

'What about their air force?' Peled asked Colonel Avi.

'There are two squadrons patrolling Iranian airspace to the west, opposite Iraq and Turkey. And another squadron opposite Kuwait. And one on the border with Afghanistan. About 70 aircraft in all. Mostly F-14s and F-5s.'

'Ground radar?'

'Still tied up with our worm.'

'So, Iranian aircraft will not have ground control assistance.'

'We believe so.'

'So if we're going to attack, now is the time to do so,' Peled concluded.

The assembled officers murmured in agreement.

'Colonel Avi, launch the second strike.'

'Yes, sir.'

Colonel Avi walked over to his consul, picked up the radiophone and said, 'Launch.'

Minutes later pilots, most of whom were lounging on folding chairs and crates beneath the camo netting, got into their jets and started their turbines. One by one, Israeli F-15s, easily identifiable by the Star of David on their tales, began to taxi down the runway.

WASHINGTON D.C.

The president's press secretary had been chosen for her mental dexterity- demonstrated during the campaign on a cable news shout fest when she debated two other panelists and the host, and triumphed- her impressive legal background, and her 40ish good looks. Svetlana Dysenko needed all these attributes and more as she fended off questions in the White House briefing room. The reporters were divided into two camps, those of the political opposition who wanted to gloat, and those of the political opposition who wanted to know what the president was going to do about Israel. President Stettler watched with Franks, and hoped Dysenko could keep it together for the duration of the briefing.

'No, no,' she said in response to a particularly obnoxious question, 'the president does not believe his agenda is rejected.'

'But how can you say that?' asked the reporter, flicking his head, causing his wavy gray hair to bounce slightly.

'I remind you, David, that both President Clinton and President Bush suffered significant midterm losses and still governed effectively.'

Someone tried to ask whether the Clinton and Bush presidencies were Stettler's template going forward, but before the question was finished, a pretty cable news reporter with a red dye job asked, 'Did the president authorize the Israeli strike?'

'The Israeli government does not need permission from the president to act,' Dysenko shot back.

'Very smart,' commented Franks. 'All she said was act, not defend, not attack.'

The press conference went on.

'Does the president think Israel is defending itself?' asked Red Dye job.

Dysenko fended off Red Dye Job's attack. 'The president believes that Israel has taken the action that it felt it needed to take.'

'But they attacked Iran first,' protested Red Dye Job.

'Iran is developing nuclear weapons. If someone was about to stab you, would you wait for them to do so before trying to defend yourself?'

Red Dye Job tried to ask another question but before she could, an aggressive blonde from another network asked, 'Did the president or anyone in the U.S. government have prior knowledge of the attack?'

She paused for a moment. 'No, the president did not have prior knowledge.'

'Which is true,' Franks said. He stood up and adjusted the belt around his considerable stomach.

'What about other government agencies and officials?' asked Aggressive Blonde.

Dysenko paused for a moment. Both Stettler and Franks watched as she decided what to say.

'Sophie's Choice,' Franks said.

'No,' replied Dysenko.

'No?' asked Aggressive Blonde.

'No.'

'I hope she's right,' said Stettler.

'She'll be fine,' Franks said. He took the remote control from the coffee table in front of the couch and switched off the TV. 'I need to talk to you, sir.'

'Oh boy,' Stettler said. The last time Franks began a sentence that way, he had a heart to heart with Stettler and talked him out of choosing the governor of Indiana, a close personal friend, as Vice President.

'This is the toughest crisis of your political career, sir.'

'I know.'

'You are going to have to find a way to work with the opposition. You are in a position of weakness, but in the coming days you can change that.'

'The Israeli-Iran crisis.'

'Yes.'

'I thought so.'

'You're a smart man, Mr. President.'

'Stop treating me like you're my Jewish uncle.'

Franks laughed. 'Aren't I?'

Stettler laughed too.

'If you handle this crisis, the story shifts. Instead of the story being: look at how horribly the president did in the midterms, the story becomes: look at how well the president managed the crisis in the Middle East.'

'Hmmmm.'

'Your presidency hinges on what you do in the next few days.'

'What would you do?'

'I know how to win elections, Mr. President. I know how to wrangle legislation out of Congress.' He gestured toward his considerable midsection. 'I know how to grease fat congressman. I can't tell you what to do in the Middle East. If you have to know what I think, I'll tell you.'

'I do.'

'My people are under attack and they are defending themselves.'

'I'm not sure I see it that way.'

Frank's eyes narrowed, 'Well, sir, you're wrong.'

'I think I understand.'

'I don't think you do, Mr. President. Go watch *Exodus*. Go watch *Cast a Giant Shadow*. Go watch *Raid on Entebbe*. Then tell me if you think I'm wrong.'

'I don't think watching a few movies is the way to get to know the region.'

'I could recommend a hundred books, but you don't have the time.'

'OK.'

'Now I've told you what I think. But I won't tell you what to do. All I can do is tell you the likely political impact of the actions you take and help you take them.'

Franks extended his hand, Stettler took it.

'Alright then,' Stettler said.

'The first thing I suggest, is reaching out to Jewish Congressional leaders and members on this matter. Dem, GOP, it doesn't matter, they're all united in their support for Israel. If you can get them on your side, or convince them you're on their side, they may be willing to work with you on some of your pet issues like…'

JERUSALEM

The prime minister knew the men and women in the Operations Center didn't like her being there, but she didn't care. She sat at a table in the middle of the room, surrounded by rows and banks of electronics, and listened in to the pilot's blow by blow account of the air battle over Iran broadcast over the center's stereo speakers.

42

The first target was Iranian combat air patrols along the western border. The task was delegated to a new formation, Talon Group, a strike force of eighteen F-15s, divided into nine groups of two. So far the score was Israel seven, Iran, zero.

'Scratch two F-5s,' reported Talon-Bet.

'And there goes another,' reported Talon-Gimell.

'This is Vet, am picking up four targets, F-14s, coming north.'

'Roger, Vet,' replied Talon-Aleph. 'Engage at your discretion.'

'Roger, Aleph.'

The two F-15s of Talon-Vet cruised south and launched a stand-off attack of eight missiles. '…missiles away…targets turning…targets running…Hit, hit!...Hit! And…hit, another down.'

'What about the last?' demanded Talon-Aleph.

'It has gone supersonic. I don't believe this. It's heading right for Iraq….yes…it's crossing into Iraq…'

Eitan watched the map of Iran shown on a large flat-screen TV. A blue blip just appeared over the Qods Force training camp in Navahand, near the Iraqi border. A technician switched to the group's radio band.

'Huge explosion, tremendous explosion,' said one of the pilots.

'Look at that barracks burn!' shouted another.

The chatter was interrupted by General Peled from his command center at Lavan, telling the pilots to shut up. They were silent, but only until the next target was hit.

'Two bombs…right on that barracks. It just exploded!'

'Coming in behind…bombs away...hit. I see one hit. That barracks went up!'

'I see people running everywhere, Simon-Aleph.'

'Away from the crater?'

'Yes.'

Opposite the large flat-screen map a dozen small TVs were tuned to various news channels. A young woman, a sergeant in the air force, sat before them with a large set of earphones. She turned around and said, 'BBC is reporting explosions in Tehran.'

'Put it up on the big screen,' ordered General Ben Zvi.

She pressed a few buttons, transferring the BBC feed to a large flat-screen above her bank of monitors.

The daytime skyline appeared. In the center of the screen was a large plume of smoke. Further beyond that was an even larger plume. An English voice narrated the scene. The male reporter said nonsensical things as he simply recounted what he saw and heard. The sound of jet engines drowned out his voice and moments later there was a large explosion in the background, a great billowing ball of yellow flame, silent until the sound reached the camera a moment later.

'Oh my God!' exclaimed the reporter. 'Martin, I think the Iranian MOD just exploded.'

'The MOD?' asked the anchor back in London. 'You mean the Ministry of Defence?'

The reporter could now be seen pressing against the railing and looking in the distance. 'Yes, yes, Martin! I think over there is where the MOD is and…' there was another scream of jet engines. 'Here they come again!' There was another ball of fire where the first one had been and another explosion. On the TV they could actually see the windows of a building in the foreground shatter with the force and sound of the explosion.

'David, how many people were in those buildings?'

'It is impossible to say, Martin,' the reporter said as the Israeli jets streaked away in the background. 'On a normal workday, thousands. Today, I don't know.'

'Were they working on this day?'

'I know the Ministry of Defence was open, that is the case.'

'My God, how many people might the Israelis have killed?' Martin asked.

Several of the officers and enlisted personnel heckled the Television.

'One moment, David, we are now going live, to Tel Aviv, for an interview with a spokesman for the Israeli so-called government. Colonel Avigdor Zev, thank you for joining us.'

'My pleasure.'

'Do you, sir, take any responsibility for the untold deaths your nation has inflicted here?'

Zev deflected the verbal barb and responded, 'My nation, the Jewish State, has taken action to prevent an attack upon it by nuclear armed mullahs.'

'By attacking civilian targets, sir?'

'I am not at liberty to discuss our military operations.'

Damn it, Eitan thought. *Don't stone wall, just tell the truth.*

'Can you see what we are monitoring?' the BBC anchor asked.

'Yes, I can.'

'That is the Iranian Ministry of Defence, home to thousands of civilian workers.'

'It was also the home to thousands of military personnel, and generals plotting the destruction of Israel.'

'So was the Pentagon.'

'The Pentagon?' replied Zev. 'Surely you are not comparing our defensive act to the 9/11 attacks?'

'Al Qaeda attacked the Pentagon, sir, and now you have attacked the Iranian Ministry of Defence.'

'I'm sorry, Martin, I don't think you're treating your viewers with much respect. Surely you know the difference between a terrorist group trying to murder civilians, and a democratic state acting in self defense. After all, the mullahs have pledged our destruction. I think the Americans, for their part, would find your remarks to be deeply offensive.'

At this point the BBC anchor was visibly upset and stuttered.

'Goal!' someone in the Operations Center shouted.

Eitan smiled to herself.

'..Yes, yes,…but....'

Before the BBC anchor could continue Colonel Zev went on. 'Now Martin, all I ask of you, and all I ask of your viewers is to ask yourselves, what would you do? The mullahs have sworn to annihilate Israel, the eternal home of the Jewish people. They are building nuclear weapons to do so. This is against international law, as you know, Martin. They have armed terrorists in Lebanon and Gaza, who rained missiles down on Israeli school children. I ask you Martin, how much of this are we to take?'

General Ben-Zvi leaned over and said into the prime minister's ear, 'If this were a fight, Colonel Avi would have won it in the first round.'

Eitan nodded her head and wrapped her knuckles on the table in agreement. 'We'll need many more like that.'

RIYADH

When Prince Abdullah returned to his office after his emergency meeting with the king, General Rafah was waiting for him.

'Cousin, as ordered by the king, all regular army units are mobilized,' said General Rafah.

'Very well.'

'What did the king say?'

Abdullah shook his head. 'He sees this as an opportunity to unify Sunni and Shia Islam.'

'That is mad.'

'It is, but there is no one who will tell the king that.'

General Rafah shook his head. 'Those advisors…'

'Yes. Those Imams and Madrassa scholars have filled the King's head with visions of Islamic unity brought about by himself. And if he can do that, he will be a legend.'

'And he believes this is the time?'

'Yes. He believes Allah has tricked the Jews into attacking Iran so that he can come to Iran's rescue. And by doing so, he takes the first step toward Islamic unification. If Shia Iran comes under our protection then so will the Shias in Iraq, Syria, and Lebanon. Once this is accomplished the Jordanians, the Egyptians, even the Turks will be too weak to oppose him.'

'What does he want you to do?'

'For now, we wait.'

'In the future?'

'I am to draw up contingency plans for an attack on Israel.'

General Rafah laughed. 'Why not?'

'I intend to start right away.'

'No.'

'Yes.' Prince Abdullah cleared his throat. 'But cousin, after those plans are submitted, it will fall to you to ensure they are never carried out.'

JERUSALEM

General Ben Zvi sat down in the prime minister's office with Eitan. Even though it was dinner time, she had not eaten and had no plans to do so.

'I'm too nervous to eat,' she told the chief of staff.

'A sensation I know well, Prime Minister.' He smiled in sympathy.

'The briefing, please,' she said. 'In a few minutes I'm to speak with the Chancellor of Germany, one of our only allies in this crisis.

General Ben Zvi smiled at the statement's irony. 'Very well. All strike groups are returning.'

'Losses?'

'So far, none.'

The prime minister slowly exhaled. 'What damage?'

'Maccabee Force obliterated the MOD, Pasdaran HQ, Revolutionary Guard HQ, and several Qods Force training camps. There is no way to know what kind of human loses we have inflicted. How many members of the leadership we have killed. That said, there is every reason to believe that their losses have been significant.'

'How so?'

'We struck during the day. We struck when we knew there was much activity around those facilities.'

'And civilians there as well.'

'Yes.'

'I don't like that,' said Eitan.

General Ben Zvi considered his words for a moment and said, 'Prime Minister, these facts are not for you to like. They are for you to consider and understand.'

Eitan didn't respond. Instead she asked, 'Does General Peled wish to proceed?'

'General Peled says that he thinks so but doesn't want to make a final decision until the pilots have been debriefed.'

'What are your thoughts, General?'

'Well…'

There was a knock on the door. One of the prime minister's aides said that one of the general's aides had an urgent message from the operations center.

'Will you excuse me, please?'

She nodded for General Ben Zvi to take his leave. He left and came back a minute later.

'Prime Minister,' said Ben Zvi, 'One of our F-16s has been shot down.'

LAVAN ISLAND

Gonzo made himself as unobtrusive as possible, observing and scribbling notes as the situation unfolded. Two Blackhawk and two Apache helicopters took off from the airstrip. They joined a quartet of F-15s and a quartet of F-16s already scrambled who would, if need be, fight their way to the downed pilot.

'Rescue Force is in the air,' said Colonel Avi.

'Is the downed pilot alive?' asked Peled.

'We can't tell,' Colonel Avi replied. 'His transponder is activated. He is about 170 miles northwest of us, outside a town named Bushgan.'

Colonel Avi highlighted the town on the map.

'That's about 50 miles from Bushehr,' said Peled.

'Yes, sir.'

'Do we have any assets over his position?'

'Just his wingman, he's covering.'

'Get him out of there. I don't want to be worrying about two downed pilots. Get him out of there right now.'

A technician superimposed the transponder signal against a Google Earth Map. They zoomed in to an altitude of about 10,000 feet. The image showed the town of Busghan in a fertile river valley. Rough mountain slopes were on either side. East of the town was a large system of irrigated fields.

'The pilot's wingman reports he saw his chute go down in these fields. His F-16 crashed on the north slope of the valley.'

'So everyone in Bushgan could see.'

'I am afraid so, General.'

'Wonderful.'

Peled looked to the flat-screen display and saw a blue dot approaching the crash site. 'What is that?' he pointed.

'Unmanned drone.'

By the time the drone was over the target, the sun was starting to go down. Rescue Force was fifteen minutes away. Peled simply stood back and let Colonel Avi conduct the operation. Chatter between Rescue Force pilots filled the air of the command center.

'There,' said the lead helicopter pilot. 'I see the downed F-16.' It was in a field about a mile southeast of Bushgan. 'There are several vehicles around it.' The pilot's transponder was still on a mile south of the crash site.

'No sign of aircraft?' asked Rescue Force Leader.

'None in your area, Rescue Force Leader, several concentrations to the north.'

'Request permission to go in, Rescue Force Leader.'

'Proceed.'

With permission to proceed Rescue Force Leader, aboard one of the Blackhawks, gave orders to his team. The four F-15s of Eagle Force, would form a perimeter while the four F-16s of Falcon Force would escort the helicopters to the crash site. As Israeli aircraft entered the valley, the situation drastically changed. Many of the Iranian Air Force contacts to the north suddenly changed course and raced south. Even worse, several new contacts, a dozen in all, appeared on the radar just north of the valley.

'New contacts, new contacts,' Peled heard over the radio.

'Am vectoring fighters to engage long range targets,' said Rescue Force Leader.

'What about those closing F-5s?' someone asked.

'Eagle Group move in and engage.'

As the Eagles acquired the long range targets and engaged, Rescue Force's F-16s went supersonic and sped out to engage the F-5s. A raging dog fight erupted in the sky over Bushgan. Peled could only listen to the radio chatter as the battle unfolded.

'Target acquired, engaging,' the pilot said dispassionately over the sound of an electronic buzz indicating a missile had acquired a target. 'Missile away…on target…hit!'

'Break starboard, Falcon -Three, break starboard…two bogies…'

'Breaking starboard and running low…'

'I got one…missile away….hit!'

'Other bogie is banking to port.'

'Not for long!' there was a ripping sound as the pilot fired his nose cannon. 'Just missed…got him…' another buzzing sound. 'Got him!'

'Falcon-One, what is the status of those long range targets?'

'Two down, six still coming. Am re-engaging.'

'Roger.'

'One bogey…missile away…hit!'

'One coming up on your six.'

'Am climbing.'

'I'm coming after him.'

'In my sights. Dive, dive!' There was the sound of excited breathing. 'That's it, site's clear, firing...' a buzzing sound, 'just clipped his tail... he's going down.'

'Two bogies closing,' said Rescue Leader. 'Keep them the hell away from my helicopters.'

There was crosstalk between pilots as an Israeli F-16 mixed it up with a pair of F-5s. Finally there was the electronic buzzing sound again and, 'Missile away....hit! Closing in on the other target...he just keeps diving...he's right off the ground...man is he illuminated...' There was a buzzing sound. 'There goes his nose...he just slammed into the ridge. New target...pursuing...'

'Falcon-Four, get back here,' ordered Falcon-One.

'Two more targets down, but they keep closing,' reported Falcon-Four. 'Two more missiles away...'

'More bogies, four more, closing in fast from the southwest.'

'Get that pilot off the ground before this area gets too hot!' ordered Rescue Force Leader.

'The area is already too hot,' replied the helo commander. 'Approaching now. I see him! He's waving. He has the rescue beacon. We're going down to get him now.'

'I see Iranian military vehicles on the road to the north,' said Apache - One.

'Engage.'

'Engaging with Hellfire missiles,' reported the pilot. 'Boom! Boom!' he said. 'Hope that guy has his car insurance paid up.'

'Stop the chatter.'

'Engaging another...got it.'

'Infrared shows people on that road, running toward our man.'

'I'm going in with my cannons,' said Apache-Two. There was a tremendous ripping sound as the pilot let loose several bursts. 'They're not heading toward our man anymore.'

'Apache-One, cover. Keep firing! Apache-Two, escort the Blackhawks in.'

'Roger.'

'Copy that.'

There was chatter between the pilots and then, 'Apache-One, I'm taking fire from the road.'

'I see it, looks like some sort of truck-mounted gun,' said Apache-One. There was another ripping sound. 'Engaged and destroyed.'

'There's another one,' shouted one of the Blackhawk pilots. 'Taking fire here.'

'Get out of there,' ordered Rescue-One.

'But the pilot…'

'We'll pick him up when the area is cleared.'

'Engaging now,' reported Apache-One.

'This is Apache-Two. Fire down below. Looks like small arms. Engaging.' They heard firing from the gunship's nose cannon. 'They're everywhere. Still firing…whoa! That was an RPG!' shouted the now excited pilot. 'I'm pulling back…there goes another RPG…these guys can't shoot.'

'Watch it, Apache-Two,' said Apache - one, 'I see another truck-mounted gun.'

'Where?!' said Apache-Two over the sound of small arms and RPG fire.

'Coming off the road, there's another truck behind it,' Apache-One fired his chain cannon. 'He's stopped.'

'Can you get them, Apache-One?' the chain cannon fired again. 'I'm dealing with these guys down here.'

'Targeted… I see guys running away from the other truck,' he let the nose cannon rip again. 'Engaging.'

'Keep at them,' said Rescue-One.

'They're running now.'

'Alright, get in there Blackhawks,' ordered Rescue Force Leader.

'Coming in now…Down, feelers out,' said the commander as commandos jumped to the ground to collect the downed pilot. 'Got him!... He's aboard!...taking off!'

Peled interjected. 'How is the pilot?'

In the background there was laughter, 'He says he wants another jet.'

'Very well. Get home.'

'Copy that.'

Rescue Force did not make directly for Lavan. Instead, as the Eagles launched one last volley of missiles to keep the pursuing Iranian jets away, they went south and didn't turn east until they were well over the Persian Gulf.

'What is the final tally, Colonel Avi?'

'Eight aircraft in exchange for our one.'

'Do we know the status of the F-16 wreck?' asked Peled.

'No.'

'Find out. If it is not completely obliterated, make sure you send a pair of F-16s to destroy it.'

For the first time, Gonzo spoke 'Why, General? Why so important to make sure they don't have a wrecked aircraft?'

'I don't want to see pictures of hooting Iranians dancing as they hoist the wreckage of one of our jets into the air. It will be a great pro-paganda victory.'

'I see.'

'The Iranian government, and the Iranian people, must see that they have completely failed. In every way. Operation Gideon Strike must be a total, absolute victory.'

Peled didn't feel relieved until the Blackhawks actually landed on Lavan Island. He visibly sighed. Taking their cue from Peled the crew in the operations center actually clapped and cheered. The helicopters landed at the end of the runway. The helicopter pilots and Sayareet Makhal commandos congratulated one another and traded notes on the mission.

As Israeli aircraft landed on Levan Island, Peled went down to the impromptu infirmary aboard one of the C-130s and met with the downed pilot. When Peled arrived, the pilot was surrounded by his squadron mates who told jokes at his expense. He had some bumps and bruises but was otherwise fine and eagerly awaited his chance to get back in the air. Peled shook the pilot's hand and congratulated him on his safe return. Gonzo got there just as Peled was leaving.

'I have to get his story, General,' he said to Peled.

'It might make an interesting book.'

Gonzo's eyes came alive, 'You know, General...'

Peled left Gonzo with that thought and returned to the command center. Colonel Avi was waiting for him. 'Drones over targets now,

General Peled.' Colonel Avi motioned toward the bank of drone pilots. He leaned over and looked at their television monitors.

The drone commander said, 'All targets extremely active.'

'How so?'

'Bunkers are open. Many vehicles coming and going. At this site here,' he pointed to one of the monitors, which showed a dark ground with dozens of orange and red spots, 'We have seen long cylindrical crates and cylinders being loaded onto trucks.'

'So they are preparing a missile launch.'

'Yes.'

Peled took his beret off and rubbed his bald head.

'Israel is about to be attacked.'

'That is my opinion.'

Colonel Avi nodded. 'Four strike groups arming and fueling now.'

'If we attack now,' Peled began, 'we can stop the Iranians from launching. We may even catch them as they're fueling their missiles.' He turned to the intel officer. 'Any indication that the Iranians are curious about us here?'

'None at all, General,' he replied.

He asked the cyber-warfare officer, 'What is the status of their communications? Their computer networks.'

'Their systems are still badly disabled, but slowly they are exterminating our bugs.'

'What does that mean?'

'It means I can no longer guarantee that their radar and communications will be disabled. Though they should still be hampered.'

'Can you rearm some F-16s to carry anti-radar missiles?'

'Within half an hour.'

'Very well. Get ready to launch.'

JERUSALEM

On the third night of the war, Major Romi Ben-Joseph became an internet sensation. To him fell the toughest public relations job: appear on al-Jazeera and make the Israeli case to the Arab world. On this night he was on opposite an Iranian government spokesmen, a severe looking bearded mullah wearing a kufa atop his head. The Iranian government spokesman began by attacking the news anchor, an older but well made and pretty woman, for even having Major Ben-Joseph on the broadcast. 'To bring this pig of the Zionist Entity into Muslim living rooms, is an abomination,' he said in passable but heavily accented Arabic.

When the mullah was finished, the anchor said, 'Major Ben-Joseph, thank you for appearing on al-Jazeera.'

The Mullah tried to speak but the anchor waved her hand, and a technician muted his mic.

'It is my pleasure to be here, Wafah,' replied Major Ben-Joseph, calling the anchor by her first name. 'I am grateful for the opportunity.'

'The pleasure is mine,' said the anchor. 'Now please, if you will, Major, tell us why Israel has launched this unprovoked attack on a Muslim country.'

'Now, hold it right there, Wafah,' said Major Ben-Joseph. 'We weren't unprovoked.'

'But Iran did not attack you.'

'But they have, Wafah. My country has been assailed by rockets and mortars manufactured in Iran. These Iranian weapons have been fired at Israeli women and children. The damage has been horrible. And mine is not the only country where Iranian weapons have done great harm.'

'But your attack…'

'If I may finish, Wafah. Iranian weapons were rampant in Iraq in the previous decade. Iranian weapons, and Iranian thugs have the blood of thousands of Iraqis on their hands. I have seen the results of those weapons first hand.'

'What do you mean, Major?'

'My training is medical. I interned at America's Walter Reed Army Medical Center. I worked personally with dozens of American servicemen, and women, Wafah, who had been horribly maimed fighting to defend an Arab country from Persian interlopers.'

'But this attack of yours on Iran, surely it has killed hundreds, if not thousands.'

'I pray it hasn't, Wafah. Because I know the price. But what choice did we have? Were we to allow the mullahs to get nuclear weapons?

You know, Wafah, there are a million Israeli-Arabs. What would be their fate if Iran were to launch a nuclear attack on Israel?'

'Israeli-Arabs?' said the anchor. 'They are second class citizens.'

'I'm sorry, Wafah, I must take issue with that. My country is not perfect, and there is a difference between the law and the actions of people, but in the eyes of the law, Israeli-Arabs are Israeli citizens.'

'That may be so, Major Ben-Joseph, but some say this action is just another Israeli attack on the Muslim world.'

'Well, Wafah, I urge those who would believe such a thing to look at the world around them. Look at the slaughter the Mullahs have perpetrated in the Arab world. Their commandos in Iraq, their henchmen in Lebanon. Their secret police helped slaughter thousands of Syrians during the late revolution there. I'm sorry Wafah, but Persian Iran has killed far more Arabs than has Jewish Israel.'

The anchor nodded for her technician to switch the Mullah's microphone back on.

'Now, sir,' she began, 'what do you have to say to Major Ben-Joseph's remarks?'

Rather than answer, the Mullah held up a computer printout of a photograph. 'Now, young miss, I have to tell you, this is how depraved the Zionist pigs are.'

'What are you holding up, sir?' asked the anchor.

'I would not subject your viewers to this except I think they should see the crimes of the Jews.'

'What is it?' the anchor asked.

'It is a photograph of an unwashed whore, exposed for the world to see. The Zionist pigs controlled our ministry of information website and put it there.'

In the al-Jazeera control room, a quick thinking technician went to the Iranian Ministry of Information website and brought the image on the view screen. It showed a bikini clad blonde woman lying on wet sand and luxuriating in the sun.

'Major Ben-Joseph?'

'Why that is Israeli supermodel Bar Refaeli.'

'Major Ben-Joseph, why would you do such a thing?'

'Well Wafah, I can only speculate. I guess our computer experts have an ironic sense of humor.'

'But this image, it could be considered by some to be offensive.'

Major Ben-Joseph smiled sheepishly, and even blushed a bit. 'Wafah, all I can say is that we in Israel love women. We love a woman's body and we celebrate it. Now maybe the Mullahs do not, but in Israel a beautiful woman such as Bar Refaeli is free to do what she wishes. As you know, in Iran...'

The Israeli ministry of information uploaded Major Ben-Joseph's al-Jazeera appearance to its YouTube account as soon as the interview was over. They titled the clip *Major Ben-Joseph vs the Mullah*. An Israeli blog, run by an Australian expat, saw the clip first and commented. From there it was picked up by several right-leaning American blogs. By midnight Drudge ran the pic of Bar Refaeli beneath the headline *Slayer of Mullahs*. The next morning the al-Jazeera clip was being aired on American morning news shows. By noon the Israeli embassy in Washington had fielded no less than two dozen calls from American women inquiring about Major Ben-Joseph's marital status.

LAVAN ISLAND

Maccabee Force fanned out over Iran in small groups. Quartets of F-15s cruised the skies and engaged Iranian air force jets. This time the Iranians scrambled their Mig-29 Fulcrums, the best jets in their fleet. Because they were not able to coordinate with ground radar the Fulcrums were fed into the ensuing fight in groups of four and eight. The Israeli F-15 pilots shot down nine before the Fulcrum squadron commanders ordered their pilots to retreat north, out of range of the Israelis. They gathered over Tehran and waited for an opportunity to rejoin the fight. At the same time, Iranian air defense systems, whose computers had finally been purged of Israeli bugs, joined the fray. As their radars went live, pairs of F-16s armed with anti-radar missiles swooped in and engaged.

At the same time, several quartets of laser guided bomb armed F-16s attacked a half dozen secondary nuclear facilities within Iran. These included the uranium mines and milling plants in the east of the country around Yazd, plus research and development facilities in the north of the country at Yonab, Tabriz, Karaj and Chalus. Efforts were also mounted against a half dozen suspected sites scattered throughout the country.

At the command center on Lavan Island, Colonel Avi kept tabs on a scorecard as one by one, Iranian missile batteries winked out.

'Hit, target hit,' reported one F-16 pilot.

The intelligence officer made a couple of slash marks on his note pad, 'That's two more S-200 sites taken out south of Tehran,' he said.

'How many altogether?' asked Colonel Avi.

'Thirteen S-200s, eleven Hawks.'

'General, I'm not sure I agree with pressing the attack on their air defence network,' said Avi.

'The more missile sites we take out now, while their systems are in disarray, the less we may have to deal with later if we have to come back.'

'Hit,' reported another F-16 pilot.

'That's another S-200, west of Tehran,' said Avi.

As the operation unfolded it was clear the Israelis completely outclassed the Iranians. The F-15 pilots downed another pair of Fulcrums and then a trio of F-5s.

'Our strike group is approaching Tabirz,' said Colonel Avi.

'Put them on.'

A tech put the pilot's radio chatter on speakers.

'Approaching now…I see flak, a wall of flak.'

'Do they know we're coming?'

Colonel Avi interjected. 'No indication. Iranian radar is still out.'

'I see tracers…explosions.'

'They're just firing blind…'

'Push through it,' ordered the flight commander.

They heard firing and explosions, then. 'I see launchers…targeting…bombs away…hit!'

'Look at that explosion!' someone said.

'Secondary's, look at those secondary explosions!'

'One missile after another going off.'

'Targeting…bombs away…'

'Hit!…'

Colonel Avi looked at Peled, 'Looks as if we caught them as they were readying to launch.'

Peled nodded. 'I don't want the pilots lingering too long over the target. Get them out of there.'

'Yes, sir.'

'Get our aircraft back, get them refueled and rearmed. I want a list of targets at Bushehr within the hour.'

'Yes, sir,' said Colonel Avi.

'After that it will be time for us to go home...'

WASHINGTON, D.C.

In the Oval Office, a half dozen people waited for President Stettler to have his first conversation with Prime Minister Eitan since Israel started the war. Franks sat on the sofas with Boddicker, Davis and Wesson. Kneeling before the president's desk was a trio of photographers from the White House reporter pool.

Stettler sat behind the desk, wearing glass. He didn't need them, but Franks insisted he sometime be photographed wearing them, to make him look wiser. On this occasion he didn't wear a blazer and had rolled his sleeves up to seem workmanlike. The light on the desk phone told Stettler that Prime Minister Eitan was waiting on the other line. They had met on two previous occasions, the meetings were formal but pleasant, but no one from either office was able to say that the two leaders had built up a friendly rapport.

Stettler looked at Franks, who stood up and waddled over to the desk.

'Remember, sir, she is addressed as Prime Minister, not Madam Prime Minister.'

'I know,' Stettler said, remembering his flub the first time he met Eitan the year before.

'Also remember after this you are meeting with a delegation of Jewish congresspersons and senators. It would be nice if you had something positive to report.'

Stettler nodded. 'OK,' he said, and waved his hand.

Franks went back and plopped down on the couch. Stettler picked up the phone. The photographers began taking photos.

'Prime Minister,' he began. 'So good of you to find a moment to call me.'

'Mr. President thank you for taking time from your busy schedule to speak with me.'

'Not at all, Prime Minister. I know that in these times…'

About five minutes into the conversation, Wesson stood up on his haunches and motioned to the president.

Franks looked askance at Wesson and said, 'Sit down.'

'Oh, Prime Minister, when this crisis has subsided I would like to talk with you about restarting the Peace Process…'

When Franks heard these words his heart sank and then he became annoyed. He flashed an angry glance at Wesson, who eagerly looked at the president. He listened carefully to what Prime Minister Eitan said in response.

"Mr. President, with all due respect, I really do not think this is the time to discuss the Peace Process.'

'Yes, Prime Minister…'

In all they spoke for 12 minutes and 37 seconds, according to Franks watch. As the two leaders wrapped up the conversation Boddicker leaned over and whispered to Franks 'It's hard work talking that much and not saying anything.'

'It is.'

'I don't know how you political guys do this all day.'

Franks looked over at Boddicker as if he'd just farted. 'What do you think you are Mr. Boddicker?'

Boddicker smirked but said nothing.

The president wished Eitan well and hung up the phone. He stood up. After the president paused for a few more photos, Franks shooed the photographers out of the Oval Office.

'How'd I do, Gary?' he asked.

'I thought the conversation went fine, Mr. President. I would have avoided mentioning the Peace Process though.'

'Hmmm…she didn't like it.'

'No, sir,' added Boddicker. 'I don't think it was the right time to bring it up.'

'Well, it is the cause of much of the region's problems,' said Wesson.

Franks was about to say something, but Stettler interrupted. 'Alright, boys, not now. OK. I have to meet a congressional delegation.'

Franks, Wesson and Davis left the Oval Office. Outside was a delegation of Jewish members of Congress. When they filed into the Oval Office, Franks turned to Wesson. 'Mr. Secretary. Don't you ever interject yourself into a presidential phone call again, clear?'

Wesson looked visibly taken aback. It took him a moment to compose himself. When he did, the secretary of state said, 'How dare you speak to me like this. I am the President's Secretary of State.'

'You are a career civil servant on his last legs. And I'm not sure the president should be taking your advice.'

'How dare you.'

'How dare I? How did your mediation efforts in Africa end? Or Burma? Or on the Mosquito coast?'

'I serve the president and----'

'You serve your own ego. You and all you do-gooders. If I did my job as badly as you do yours, I'd get out of the business.'

Davis, like a man who had already faced Frank's wrath, simply averted his gaze.

In the Oval Office, the leader of the congressional delegation, a senator from Illinois said, 'Mr. President, our delegation is concerned about the strength of your support for Israel in this crisis.'

'How so, Senator?'

'Well, as you know, the Arab League is pushing for the UN to condemn the strike. Egypt has proposed the resolution and so far, more than two dozen nations have signed on.'

A congressman from California spoke next. 'Mr. President, why hasn't your administration promised to veto this?'

'Well, after consulting with Secretary Wesson...'

CHAPTER IV

MACCABEE'S FALLOUT

Operation Gideon Strike has been compared to the Osirak raid, Entebbe, and even Pearl Harbor. It is not for me to judge where Operation Gideon Strike falls in the pantheon of air warfare. But here are the facts. We delivered a blow to the Mullah's nuclear program from which they have not recovered. Decades of research and work were burned up in the flames or buried beneath the rubble. Hundreds of billions of dollars are gone forever. Additionally, Operation Gideon Strike destroyed their entire mid-level military and terrorist infrastructure. We killed hundreds of officers and intelligence operatives, greatly impeding the Mullah's ability to make war and terror abroad. We smashed their entire command and control infrastructure. Maccabbe Force shot down sixty three Iranian aircraft and all but annihilated their air defense network.

Truly Operation Gideon Strike was a great success...

Three Missions,

General Benny Peled

OVER SAUDI ARABIA

The sands of Saudi Arabia passed beneath General Peled's now airborne command center. Every aircraft in Gideon Strike was in the air. The C-130s, drones, and helicopters made their way back to Israel, while Maccabee Force struck one last target. Back on Lavan, the SAM battery launchers had been spiked, the runway cratered, and the Iranian prisoners released. Oman had been scuttled in the port.

'We're picking up al-Jazeera's signal, sir,' said Colonel Avi. He pointed to one of the TV monitors. 'They have a camera crew on the ground at Bushehr.

'I want to see.'

He put on a pair of headphones and watched the al-Jazeera broadcast. The reporter and camera crew were on the ground not more than a mile southeast of the reactor. The image showed the plant in the background. The buildings around the cooling tower were aflame, while the top of the tower itself seemed to have been sheared off. Smoke billowed from the cooling tower as if it were a volcano. There were dozens of flashes of light on the ground and streaks of light arcing through the air as the assembled Iranian anti-aircraft guns fired blindly. The left side of the screen showed a burning Iranian corvette. Silhouetted by the firelight was another corvette, listing badly to starboard. Over the talking of the al-Jazeera reporter Peled heard the scream of jet engines, a whistling sound and then a flash of light which blinded the TV screen for a second. When the image returned, Peled could see a great smoldering hole in the side of the cooling tower. He spoke passable Arabic and was able to follow the anchor.

'I can tell you, Wafah, that a great aerial battle has been waged overhead. With my own eyes I saw several Zionist jets crash into the gulf.'

Peled looked at Colonel Avi, who shook his head. 'Not ours,' he said.

'How long has the battle overhead been waged, Abdul?'

'At least one half hour...look!' said the reporter, who pointed toward the sky.

The camera panned up and showed a flaming aircraft streaking across the sky.

'Is that Iranian or Zionist?' the anchor asked.

'I cannot tell, Wafah.'

Peled turned to Colonel Avi, 'What is the tally so far?'

Colonel Avi looked at his note pad. 'Thirteen Iranian aircraft down. Including three Fulcrums. They're coming at Maccabee Force in waves.'

'Good.'

'It would seem we've drawn the Iranian air force into a massive battle on our terms.'

Al-Jazeera showed another explosion on the ground, and then another and another. There were sonic booms overhead and then more flashes of light, a quick succession on the ground until a great orange cloud of fire erupted from Bushehr.

'They breached the containment dome,' said Colonel Avi.

There was another series of explosions as Israeli F-16s made another pass at the dome. One final blast shattered the entire structure and collapsed the dome in on itself.

There were screams and exclamations from the reporter and then the image went black as the camera crew dropped their equipment and ran.

'General?' asked an airman. 'We've reached Point Xray. Shall we drop the debris?'

Peled nodded. He moved forward to the cockpit where he could see one of the strike force's C-130s. The aft cargo door opened. Peled could see an airman holding on to a handle by the door. Behind him were two other airmen. The deck sergeant nodded and the airmen grabbed pieces of wrecked fuselage and threw them out of the plane. Peled watched as they tossed part of the wing of an F-16 and then the tail, bits of nose and canopy, and then the nose cone of an F-15, all conspicuously sported the Star of David. Standing behind General Peled, Gonzo wondered why they would drop debris from a pair of Israeli jets onto the Saudi desert.

WASHINGTON D.C.

The First Lady was at a charity benefit and Kelly had not yet returned from her MTV set. So at a quarter to eleven, Stettler had the White House residence all to himself. He sat on the couch in front of the TV, trying to get his personal laptop to work. Growing up in the woods and the outdoors, he had never had a great feel for technology, and the myriad of codes and procedures one had to go through to use the internet from the White House had defeated Stettler.

He was about to concede when Kelly walked in. Stettler looked at his daughter. Her TV hair and makeup were still on. She wore boots, tights, and a form fitting shirt that did not cover her posterior. Stettler didn't really like seeing his daughter this way, but her mother had said, 'Scot, she's seventeen, not seven.'

'How was the show?' he asked.

'Fine,' Kelly replied. She headed straight for her room.

'How was school?'

'Fine.'

'Kelly, could you stop for a moment?'

She turned around. 'Yeah.'

'Could you help with this?' He nodded toward the computer.

Kelly sighed. 'Again?'

'Your mother isn't here.'

She walked over to the couch, sat down, and took the laptop. She furiously tapped the keyboard, hit return, tapped it again and hit return again. The screen went blank and blinked for a few seconds. Then the screen showed the website Stettler had wanted, YouTube.

A movie started. It was a grainy film, showing an airport lounge.

'God, look at those clothes,' Kelly said.

'Ahh, the 70's.' Stettler pointed to the screen. 'Your mother wore a dress like that on our first date.'

'Ewwww...' Kelly said as she saw a Jewish-looking man with an afro and a yellow, butterfly collared shirt. 'Oh my God! Look at that guy!'

Kelly sat down on the couch and watched the unfolding horror of 70's fashion. She stayed and watched *Raid on Entebbe* for nearly half an hour before her cell phone beeped with a new text message which she absolutely had to answer. It was more time than Stettler had spent alone with his daughter in a year.

The next morning he was in a good mood, until he turned on the TV and saw the lead news story about the Israeli strike on Bushehr.

At the first morning briefing with Franks, Stettler asked, 'Are they done? Please tell me they're done.'

'Assuming Ambassador Silber's report is accurate, then the Israelis are finished,' said Franks.

The TV in the Oval Office was tuned to BBC, which showed aerial images of the inferno that was the Bushehr nuclear plant. On the bottom of the screen ran the headline 'Nuclear Nightmare?' The BBC anchor was in high dungeon about the potential nuclear and environmental catastrophe the Israelis had unleashed.

Franks said, 'At least when they hit Osirak in '81, the plant wasn't online yet.'

The image switched from the Bushehr plant to the news anchor. Behind him was an image of the US Capitol with the headline, *Political Fallout: International*. Stettler was more worried about the political repercussions of the Israeli strike at home. All morning the White House switchboard had been lit up by phone calls. Thousands of them urging Stettler to veto the impending UN Resolution condemning Israel. It was a coordinated campaign sponsored by a dizzying array of Jewish groups from the New Israel Fund to the Emergency Committee for Israel, the Republican Jewish Coalition and Christians United for Israel, all demanding the president act in defense of Israel.

'If I let that UN resolution through?'

'Then the Jewish members of Congress will crucify you, pardon the pun.'

'How many again?'

'Thirty three house members and eight senators.'

'So I can forget the domestic issues I was going to work with them on.'

'Essentially.'

'And if I veto the resolution, I'll take hell abroad.'

'So Wesson tells us.'

'And the vote's tomorrow.'

Franks didn't reply.

'I'd like a cabinet meeting tonight.'

RIYADH

Prince Abdullah hung up the phone.

'The king is demanding an emergency meeting,' Abdullah said to General Rafah.

'He has met with the Iranian ambassador?'

'Yes. If this cabinet meeting happens, it is going to be very hard to carry out our plan.'

'I have multiple teams in the desert now. All personally loyal to me. When is the meeting?'

'Tonight,' said Abdullah.

General Rafah thought for a moment. 'If we have not found the site by the meeting, I will order an air raid alert.'

'Excellent idea.'

'The king's ministers won't travel if they think Zionist jets are in the air.'

'That might buy your teams enough time to find the debris.'

'And then we show it to the world.'

WASHINGTON D.C.

At the president's request, the lights had been dimmed in the situation room. Even so, the light cast by the lamps seemed like daggers in his eyes. As the meeting went on, Stettler's headache only got worse.

'Mr. President,' concluded Boddicker, 'It looks as if the Israelis drew the Iranian air force into a trap around Bushehr.'

'Is that why they waited so long to attack it?'

'I believe so. We can't say with certainty the extent of the casualties the Israelis inflicted upon the Iranians. But, listening to al-Jazeera broadcasts, I would think they downed as many as two dozen aircraft.'

Wesson cleared his throat and spoke. 'Mr. Boddicker, I am far more concerned with the fallout, literally the fallout of the Israeli strike on Bushehr.'

'What do we know?' asked Stettler.

'It appears to be an unfolding nuclear disaster. The Israelis destroyed the electrical plant, the cooling tower and the containment dome.'

'They may have caused a meltdown. There are massive spikes in radiation levels,' said Wesson.

'So the Iranians tell us,' replied Boddicker.

'You don't believe them?' Wesson asked.

'Do you?'

Stettler held out his hands, 'Alright, gentlemen.'

Wesson persisted, 'I'm sorry Mr. President, but the Israeli strike has added an environmental catastrophe on top of a diplomatic crisis.'

Finally, Abby Benard, the Ambassador to the UN spoke, 'He's right, Mr. President.' Nearing 50, and having just flown down from New York, the Ambassador looked her age. 'The Iranians and the Arab League are preparing a stiff resolution condemning Israel. There is even wording calling for sanctions.'

'That is not acceptable to the United States,' said Stettler.

'My people have been working all day to negotiate the sanctions wording out of the resolution, but it doesn't look good. The Russians are with them, so are Spain and Italy.'

'Oh, the fearsome Spanish and Italians,' Boddicker mocked.

'France will come along as well.'

'Why haven't they already?' Stettler asked.

'Making it look good.'

'The Germans?' asked Stettler.

'Will abstain.'

Wesson shook his head.

'Can you blame them?' Boddicker asked.

'What about the British?' the president asked.

'Still making up their minds.'

Stettler closed his eyes and said, 'What happens if we veto the resolution?'

Franks spoke, 'If you veto the resolution, you begin your political comeback.'

Wesson spoke, 'Oh come on Franks, how many Jews are in America, six million?'

'Yes. About the same number as in Israel.'

'Whoops,' said Boddicker, 'There's that number again.'

Wesson shot Boddicker an icy stair. If it bothered him, Boddicker didn't show it.

'We must also consider,' said Franks, 'the support for Israel within the evangelical community. Many see it as their religious duty to support the Jews.'

'Preposterous,' said Wesson.

Boddicker laughed. 'Don't tell that to my daddy. He used to send them a hundred dollars a year. Still buys pizza for Israeli soldiers.'

Stettler raised his voice. 'OK. Ambassador Benard, what will be the fallout at the UN if we veto?'

Benard shook her head. 'In that case, I would expect the unexpected from the Iranians and the Arab League. A lot of Lawfare work from European NGOs, and maybe from some governments. I would expect the Belgians to take action in their courts.'

'Can they do that?' asked Stettler.

'The Belgians claim universal jurisdiction,' Boddicker explained. 'They may even come after you.'

Stettler thought aloud. 'I could accept a resolution condemning, but not one calling for sanctions…'

'Mr. President-' Wesson began.

'Do not interrupt,' said Franks.

'Work like hell to get the sanctions language out. Explain to them, if it stays in, we veto.'

'And if it stays in?' Wesson asked.

'I said, we veto.'

RAMAT DAVID

Peled should have felt elated to be back on the ground in Israel but instead, as he watched the pilots of Gideon Strike file into the hanger at Ramat David, he felt sick to his stomach. Peled sat on the hastily erected stage behind the podium. At that moment he would rather have been any place else. He looked out on the pilots, ground crew, and commandos, all still in the clothes they wore when

Operation Gideon Strike began 78 hours before. He felt especially bad for the Eagle and Falcon pilots who landed at Tel Nof, only to be ordered onto a transport and flown up to Ramat David. They were unshaven, unkempt, and tired. *These men and women need to be at rest*, he thought. In the front row, where his pilots should have been, sat reporters from the *Jerusalem Post, Haaretz, Ynet,* and other news outlets. A camera was in front of the dais. It panned out on the assembled military personnel while a news reporter talked, setting the scene for viewers before the prime minister arrived. She was late, to build audience at home, no doubt. When she arrived the assembled soldiers and airmen stood at attention. She strode across the stage and took the podium.

'People of the world,' she began. 'In these last days, the State of Israel has done what it had to do. The Jewish state took defensive action against a genocidal regime bent on the destruction of the Jewish people. We have attacked the tools with which that regime sought to destroy us...' she listed the various nuclear sites before going into detail about attacks on military infrastructure, 'We also attacked Qods Force, an Iranian state terrorist group which has the blood of thousands on its hands, a terrorist group which attacked synagogues around the world, killed thousands of Arabs in nations like Lebanon, and even American soldiers in Iraq...' She went on for some time in this vein, concluding. 'By attacking Iranian Qods Force, the Pasdaran and the Ministry of Defence, we have taken defensive action against those who would do us harm...'

Watching in the Oval Office, Franks turned to the president and said, 'Mentioning Qods, and all those Americans they killed in Iraq was a nice touch.' He had been admiring the craftsmanship of the event since it began, the way Eitan was there to greet the returning pilots, the drama of the speech being given at the airbase in front of the men and women who carried out the strike...Stettler was about to say something but Franks shushed him.

'...and now I would like to take a moment to thank, on behalf of the Israeli people, the government of the United States, for its courageous veto of United Nations Resolution 2016 condemning Israel for defending itself...'

'Well, I suppose that was nice of her,' Stettler said.

69

Sitting next to Peled was one of Eitan's political consultants. Peled glanced at the man, a well made and appointed professional in his late thirties, Peled had seen him on TV before. The man watched the speech from his IPhone. Peled looked at the phone and saw one of the cameras was panning across the hanger, showing the assembled military personnel. *Goddamn it,* he thought, *they're showing the faces of my pilots. Whatever happened to security?*...He grunted and said to the politico, 'Menachim Begin would never have tolerated this...'

'Huh?' said the consultant.

'Was this show your idea?' Peled whispered.

'In fact, it was.'

'You're a fool.'

'How so, General?'

'These people should be resting, and preparing.'

'Preparing for what?'

Peled rolled his eyes. 'Good god, man. Do you think about anything other than the next opinion poll? What do you think Iran is going to do when it gets its feet back under it?'

The politico looked at Peled but said nothing.

'What can you be thinking?' demanded Peled. 'That we have won the war?'

'Judging by the damage we inflicted, yes.'

Now Peled grew angry. 'What do mean, we?'

'I'm sorry, I...'

'Shut up. There are 50,000 Iranian and Syrian made rockets just a few miles from here in Lebanon. The war has only just begun...'

WASHINGTON DC

'Are you sure, Secretary Wesson?' asked the president.

'I am, sir,' replied Wesson.

'I wish you would reconsider.

'I resign reluctantly, Mr. President, but I'm afraid I cannot support your policy on the current crisis in the Middle East.'

'I need experienced diplomats, Mr. Wesson. The Iranians and the Arab League are planning an entire series of anti-Israeli resolutions this week, and I can't count on European support on this. At least not now.'

'No, sir,' said the unmoved former secretary.

Stettler sighed. 'Your decision is final?'

'It is.'

'Would you at least recommend a replacement?'

'I feel Ambassador Benard is up to the task.'

'Very well then,' said Stettler. The two shook hands, and Stettler walked Wesson out of the Oval Office.

Stettler closed the door and sat down on the one of the couches in front of his desk. He looked up at the ceiling and held a hand to his temple. Franks came in.

'My headache is back,' said Stettler.

Franks sat down across from the president.

'The press,' began Stettler, 'is going to kill me with this story.'

'Yes they are.' Franks held up the morning edition of the *Washington Post* and opened to the editorial section. 'There are two op-eds in here this morning, both praising you for your veto of Resolution 2016.'

'Who?'

'The usual suspects. And I was just watching the morning cable news shows. Senator Gold was on three of them this morning, praising you.'

'And that should be the story this morning, not Wesson's resignation.'

Franks paused for a second, feeling the president's frustration as his own. 'Wesson is an old fool who thinks there is no dispute that cannot be solved through conflict resolution theory.'

There was a knock on the door. One of Franks' assistants stuck his head in and said, 'Excuse me, Mr. President, but I thought you and the chief would want to know that there are air raid sirens going off in Riyadh.'

'Riyadh?' said Stettler.

'Yes, sir,' nodded the aide. He held up his IPhone. 'I have it right here if you want to see, sir.'

'No thanks.' Stettler reached for the remote control and turned on the TV. It was already on Fox, and showed a grainy image of the Riyadh skyline. A news reporter spoke, telling how suddenly air raid sirens had gone off, sending people in the streets scrambling indoors, and causing dozens of car accidents. The sirens had been going off for at least ten minutes.

'Why would they attack Saudi Arabia?' asked Stettler.

Franks shrugged. 'I know political strategy, not military.' Franks sat up. 'Now Mr. President, we need to schedule a series of high profile meetings between you, the cabinet, delegations from Congress…'

Stettler rubbed his temples, 'I know.'

'We need to present you as in charge of this crisis and working to resolve it.'

'I know.'

'With good optics we can begin your political resurrection…'

Stettler wasn't really listening to Franks anymore. Instead he heard the air raid siren on TV, and wondered how much worse the crisis could get.

JERUSALEM

The mood inside the cabinet room was dark. The assembled ministers, each wearing a severe expression, looked on as Minister Alon gave his report on the current diplomatic situation. He did not read from notes but spoke from memory.

'The International Atomic Energy Agency reports severe radiation contamination in and around the Bushehr site. The assessment of the world media has been brutal. The BBC, for example is calling Bushehr the new Chernobyl. In London, thousands of protestors tried to storm our embassy. In Belgium, various NGOs filed charges against you personally, Prime Minister. The Hague is already looking into war crimes charges against you, as well as General's Ben Zvi and Peled. In short, Prime Minister, Israel has never been as isolated as it is right now. Only the veto of the United States keeps us from being completely isolated. The Canadian government is supporting us as well.'

'What of the UN?' Eitan asked.

'This week, Iran, the Arab League, and the Organization of Islamic Cooperation are planning a series of resolutions. These include a resolution condemning our attack on Iran, a resolution calling for economic sanctions against Israel, and a resolution boycotting Israeli business world wide.'

'Who is supporting these resolutions besides?'

'Britain, France, Russia, there is also strong support in South American, led by Argentina.'

'The Chinese?' asked Eitan.

'Waiting, for now.'

'What of India?'

'Given that they have the same concerns about Muslim nuclear weapons as we, they have said very little about the resolutions proper, but have spoken publicly about the need to take preemptive action against Islamic extremists.'

'So we might find support there.'

'Maybe,' said the minister of foreign affairs.

'Very well. What of the Arab World?' asked Eitan.

'Large protests in Egypt, of course. The Jordanians have withdrawn their ambassador in protest. The King's advisors inform our staff in Amman that while they are deeply distraught- their words, Prime Minister- they don't intend to take any action. Yesterday, in Istanbul, half a million people protested. In Syria the Interim Revolutionary Council is encouraging rallies in all major cities.'

'Of course,' said minister of defence Levi, 'It distracts from the problems of the new regime.'

'There was rioting in Indonesia and Malaya.'

'That makes sense,' Levi dryly remarked.

'In Italy, protestors are calling for a boycott of Jewish business. Yesterday in Belgium, several supermarkets were stormed by protestors, who took Israeli produce and cheese off the shelf and urinated upon them. In Spain, the Real Madrid football team took the field against Barcelona wearing Iranian flag armbands. At the French Open, our own tennis team was booed off the court before a single serve was made.'

'So we are almost entirely alone.'

'Yes.'

'What diplomatic action do you suggest?' asked Eitan.

'At the moment, we are cultivating our relationship with India like mad. The U.S., Canada, India; that is a powerful diplomatic trio.'

'What of Brazil?' asked Eitan. 'In opposition to Argentina.'

Alon shook his head. 'That government is too left wing, they are with the Argies on this.'

'What of the Saudis?' asked Eitan.

'The new king is spitting vinegar and fire. Their television imams are a sight to see.'

'As expected.'

We know he has ordered the military to mobilize. But it has not yet done so. Not completely.'

'So, so far, the Prince's plan is in motion.'

'Yes. Now turning to domestic issues. Prime Minister, you have never been so popular. YNet conducted a poll, and 78% of the voting public approves of the attack on Iran, and 66% approve of your handling of the crisis.'

As Prime Minister Eitan made plans to expand the war, Colonel Avigdor Zev sat quietly in the BBC television studio in Tel Aviv, while in London a television anchor hosted two guests who took turns lambasting Israel for its strike on Iran. One guest, a columnist for the *Guardian,* spent two minutes calling the strike a war crime and called upon NATO to move forces to the eastern Mediterranean for an eventual attack on Israel. The other, the editor of the British Arab language newspaper, *al Arabiya*, advocated the complete destruction of Israel and hoped that 'the Jews would finally feel the wrath of the Muslim world.' Finally, the anchor quieted down the two guests.

'Colonel Zev, what do you have to say for yourself and Israel?'

'Well, Martin. Let me first thank you for having me on your program.'

'I think under the circumstances it's appropriate to have a member of the Zionist regime on.'

Colonel Zev paused for a moment before speaking. 'I want you and your viewers to know the facts. The Iranian government was building nuclear weapons for the express purpose of destroying Israel, the Jewish state, the only home and refuge of the Jewish people--'

'There are some who would dispute that.' said Martin.

'Really, Martin? Who? Who disputes that Iran was building nuclear weapons? Who disputes that they would destroy Israel?'

Martin tried to speak but Colonel Zev kept talking.

'The Iranian regime expressly targeted Haifa, Tel Aviv, even Jerusalem for destruction. I ask you Martin, and I ask your viewers this one question. What would you do? What would *you* do?'

PART II
THE CEDARS OF
LEBANON

CHAPTER I

THE CALM

The efforts of myself and other Israeli spokespersons were critical to the diplomatic effort during and after the war. Most of Europe was lost of course, but because we went on international television, public opinion in several key nations was swayed in favor of Israel. These included many of the English speaking nations, Canada and Australia, and much of the Pacific rim. Japan was of course sympathetic as was South Korea for obvious reasons. India, too came around to our side. Actually, I think our attack on Iran gave the Indians some big ideas.

Talking War,

Major Romi Ben Joseph

Executive Branch leakers, specifically the former Secretary of State, have tried to portray the president as weak and indecisive. This is crap, pure and simple. President Stettler acted with circumspection and caution, not indecision. He valued the opinion of the cabinet, and never acted without hearing all available facts and gathering many opinions.

Had the former Secretary of State acted in this manner, he would not now be providing commentary on a second rate cable network known as a haven for has-been politicians and unemployable anchors.

Crisis and Victory, Gary Franks,

White House Chief of Staff

JERUSALEM

On the fifth night of the war the streets around the prime minister's residence were mostly empty, as were the streets in all the cities of Israel. The nation's reservists stayed close to home, their uniforms and equipment, for what most pundits in Israel felt was the inevitable call-up. Everyone else, mindful of Hezbollah's vast arsenal of short and medium ranged rockets remained indoors as much as possible. Most who did venture outside did so with gasmasks. Many carried weapons. Suspicious eyes had been cast on Israel's one million Arabs. Extra police had been detailed to patrol their neighborhoods in case of anti-Arab violence. The prime minister's office had already issued a pair of strong statements decrying violence against Israeli Arabs, who after all were full-fledged citizens of the Jewish State.

Over the last five days Home Front Command had been busy. Thousands of concrete tubes, originally designed for water and sewage, but large enough for a dozen people to stand in, had been deployed throughout the country. Bus shelters had also been hardened. People were advised to seal a room in their home against biological and chemical attack. Civil defense personnel had conducted several drills, one of which caused a national panic, and led to a political firestorm causing the head of Jerusalem Home Front Command to resign.

Against this fearful backdrop Prime Minister Eitan met with her war cabinet, including Alon, Levi, Shoal, General Ben Zvi and the head of Mossad. Eitan looked at the head of Mossad and asked, 'Director Sedor, has the Saudi Prince contacted you?'

'He has and reports everything is proceeding according to plan.'

Eitan held his gaze for a moment.

'You are worried, Prime Minister.'

'No, just skeptical.'

'You do not trust him.'

'Not in the slightest.'

'He approached me, Prime Minister. He came to me. He suggested overflying Saudi air space.'

'And you do trust him,' stated the prime minister.

'We went to American University together.'

Eitan waved her hand. 'Enough...What do we know about the situation in Iran?'

'Prime Minister, there is complete panic in the Iranian government. Many are convinced Gideon Strike could not have succeeded without significant help from the inside. The president, The Mullahs, and most high ranking government officials are in hiding. As for damage to Revolutionary Guards, Pasdaran, and military infrastructure, their headquarters have been destroyed. We know that hundreds of midlevel and upper-midlevel officers, managers, and administrators have been killed.'

'Does this explain their lack of activity in the Gulf, in Lebanon?' Eitan asked.

'At least partially,' said Sedor.

'Also, I think they are taking a wait and see approach,' Alon added.

'Do any of you think the Iranians will do nothing?' Eitan asked.

The assembled men shook their heads.

'Lebanon?' she asked.

They nodded.

Eitan looked to the defence minister, 'What is the state of the armed forces?'

'All regular army units are on alert. All reservists have been notified,' said Levi.

'But not mobilized?' asked Eitan.

'No,' said Levi. 'But they can report to their units within 12 hours. Within 24 hours reserve brigades will be able to take the field.'

'Regular army deployments?'

'We have one division, 366, on alert in the south, keeping an eye on Gaza and if need be, Egypt.'

'Pray God that won't be necessary,' said Eitan.

'In Central Command the four brigades of the Judea/Samaria Division are prepared if need be, to combat Fatah and PA forces.'

'Are they really a threat?' asked Eitan.

General Ben Zvi spoke for the first time. 'Not in the field, no.'

'But terrorism,' Eitan said.

'Yes,' replied Ben Zvi.

Eitan looked at Sedor. 'Is there any indication they are planning anything?'

Sedor shook his head. 'Fatah, Islamic Jihad, PFLP, all keeping their heads down. And all the Hamas operatives within the Palestinian Authority were thrown in jail months ago.'

'General Ben Zvi, what about Northern Command?' Eitan asked.

'On the coast Division 91, two brigades plus the Paratroopers Brigade. In the center, Division 36, two brigades plus the Givati, Nahal and Kfir Brigades. In the northeast, opposite the Golan, Division 162, four brigades plus one airborne and one reconnaissance battalion, in reserve. The Golani Brigade is under the direct control of Northern Command. In all, twelve brigades deployed north. Eight brigades to deal with Hezbollah four and half in reserve.'

'General,' asked Eitan. 'Why not send Division 162 into Lebanon with Divisions 91 and 36?'

'Because it's just possible the Syrians might jump in.'

'Do you believe they will do so?'

'No, but I would be a fool if I did not prepare for such a contingency.'

'Why, in your opinion, might they intervene?' asked Eitan.

'If they feel we are violating a redline of theirs. If there is pressure from the Arab/Muslim world. Or maybe the Interim Revolutionary Council will want to consolidate control and distract from troubles at home...'

'Wonderful,' said Eitan.

'Now, Prime Minister, as to Lebanon, our plan: it has three phases, the first is Operation Break Their Bones--'

Eitan smiled. She recalled the great battles on the Sinai, and Moshe Dayan's pledge to 'Break Their Bones' even as the Egyptian army advanced onto the peninsula against the surprised IDF. 'Break Their Bones! After Dayan?'

'Yes.' There was nervous laughter.

Shoal snorted but said nothing.

'This plan,' said Sedor, 'I am concerned that once again we will fight a war against a terrorist entity, but leave its leadership intact.'

'Can we kill or capture all of their leaders, General?' Eitan asked.

'We can only try,' replied General Ben Zvi.

'What are your specific targets?' asked Eitan.

'The secretary general, of course.'

Shoal snorted again.

'Their executive council, their various regional military leaders.'

'What about their military head?' said Sedor.

'Do they even have one?' asked Eitan.

'Yes,' replied Sedor.

'What do we know about him?'

'Almost nothing,' replied Sedor.

'Then how do you know he exists?' asked Shoal.

'Military organizations need leaders,' Sedor replied. 'Also, we have intercepted communications, very low level messages, making reference to a supreme military commander known only as the Hornet.'

'The Hornet?'

'Yes.'

'I wonder how he got that name?' Eitan asked sarcastically.

'We have put together a profile of who we think it could be,' said Sedor.

'Speculation,' said Shoal.

'Yes, but informed speculation. We worked with the American FBI.'

'Alright,' said a skeptical Eitan, 'Who is he?'

'Undoubtedly a veteran Hezbollah man. Probably goes all the way back to the Lebanese Civil War. Saw fighting in other areas of Jihad, Somalia, Yugoslavia and Chechnya for sure.'

'How can you be sure?'

'Jihadis gravitated there in the 90s. He probably earned his name for being a good fighter, and vicious as well. Chechen, Bosnian, Afghan,

83

not to mention Hezbollah fighters can, as you all know, be extremely cruel. That's what we think.'

'Can you find him?' asked Alon.

'We of course, have a sophisticated electronic data gathering apparatus. There are few electronic signals in Lebanon that we cannot read. There is also our own human intelligence. I'd prefer not to go into great detail, but we have a vast spy network in the country. So we are looking.'

'Alright,' said Eitan, 'Let us say we destroy Hezbollah on the ground and we kill or capture their leadership. Does that mean we win? If not how do we define winning in this case?'

General Ben Zvi took a breath and said, 'That is up to you politicians.' He looked to Eitan, 'How do we define victory?'

Shoal spoke, 'Yes, Prime Minister. How *would you* define victory?'

I don't know, she didn't say.

NORTHERN ISRAEL

Gonzo hadn't slept in two days. As soon as Peled's plane landed at Ramat David he filed a story about General Peled called *Ice Cold Commander*. He filed a second story about the pilots he interviewed, written on the plane ride back to Israel. A third story on Lavan Island and its facilities he had written in the car on the way to the Lebanese border. Of course, all three had to be cleared with the military sensor. From there the army had teamed him up with a press liaison named Gilden who arranged a tour of the northern border.

Gilden took him to Metulla, a spit of Israeli land surrounded on three sides by territory controlled by Hezbollah. Metulla's civilians had been evacuated and the town was now garrisoned by a battalion of Israeli troops. Gonzo had been there for a day. After the exhilaration of Operation Gideon Strike, the previous 24 hours had been among the most boring of his life. Metulla was eerily calm, as was Lebanon just a few feet away on the other side of the fence from where Gonzo stood. He saw tree lined hills and Lebanese villages, and even some people. They acted completely normally until Gonzo took a photo of a man walking through a field about one hundred yards inside Lebanon. When Gonzo did this the man stopped, took his own photo of Gonzo, and walked on. Gonzo waved but the man did nothing.

'He's Hezbollah,' said the army lieutenant walking him and Gilden along the border.

There were signs of Hezbollah on the other side of the border. The road running along the border was lined with placards bearing the yellow and green Hezbollah banner. And Gonzo had to admit the picture presented on the Lebanese side of the border of peaceful towns and green fields seemed just a touch too perfect, almost like a Lebanese version of a Norman Rockwell painting. Gonzo noted this to the lieutenant.

'How much Hezbollah do you think is up there?' He motioned toward the low rising hill, less than a kilometer away, atop which stood a cluster of houses.

'Plenty. At least a few of those houses are bunkers. All are packed with weapons.'

'But I've seen children and families come out of those houses.'

'That is correct. In the coming conflict---'

'You sure there will be a conflict?'

'I've been pulling duty up here for two years,' said the lieutenant. ' I've watched Hezbollah all that time. There has to be a conflict. Anyhow, in the coming conflict Hezbollah will use the Lebanese as human shields. Any civilians we kill will be a huge victory for them. Great propaganda. The last time we went into Lebanon, in 2006, we had to stop operations for a few days after an airstrike killed dozens.'

Gonzo, who sensed he finally found a story, began taking copious notes. 'So how do you attack Hezbollah without killing civilians?'

'Very carefully,' interjected Gilden.

'Seriously.'

'We can minimize the risk but we can't eliminate it,' said the lieutenant.

'Are there any restrictions on your actions?'

'I am not at liberty to say.'

'What kind of resistance do you expect if you cross the border?'

'If?' the lieutenant asked. 'It's no secret that Hezbollah has anti-tank rockets and mortars. Thousands of trained fighters, all organized into platoons and companies.'

'What about the Lebanese Army?'

'We don't know what they will do.'

Gonzo had read a story on his Blackberry from the Lebanese Daily Star, in which the Lebanese prime minister swore to defend sovereign Lebanese territory against any external threat.

'And the 10,000 UN Peace Keepers in Lebanon?'

The lieutenant shrugged.

Gilden interrupted, 'Almost time for lunch. Come on, we'll pray together.'

Gonzo shrugged. 'I don't really practice.'

'You're on the Lebanese border on the eve of war and you can't even say a prayer?' He grabbed Gonzo by the wrist. 'Come on. It will do you some good.'

NORTH BEIRUT

The Hornet made his headquarters at a non-descript seaside villa on the northern outskirts of the city. There was nothing military about the villa's exterior which had a pool overlooking the beach and a small cabana. The Hornet slept in the cabana and swam laps in the pool every morning. The villa was a small, middleclass affair with a kitchen, a dining room and a few bedrooms. The interior was simply and modestly furnished. In one bedroom was a telephone attached to a single land-line which ran out of the villa to a relay station to the north in Tripoli; the villa's only means of communication. There were no cell phones, no internet connection, not even a computer, just this single, simple old fashioned land-line. The second bedroom was kept for the Hornet's maid, an old woman who lived in the villa full time. The property was in fact, hers, purchased for her at the Hornet's insistence. The dining area had a large table capable of seating ten people.

On the table were several maps, one of Lebanon exclusively south of the Litani, another of the Beqaa Valley, several maps of strategic towns and another of Beirut. On the wall at the head of the table was a large map of Lebanon. It was dotted with red pins marking the position of Hezbollah's one thousand launchers and maroon pins marking the location of their cash of 40,000 missiles. Another 500 yellow pins marked the positions of the Resistance Army's force of nearly 10,000 fighters. Each was organized into sectors, which were under the command of one trusted subordinate, known only by a name chosen from past Muslim warriors, Saladin, Zengi, and the like. Blue markers showed UN positions.

On this morning, like all mornings, the Hornet awoke with the sun. After rising he put on a pair of cotton pajamas and walked down to the beach. At the water's edge he said his morning prayers. When he was finished the Hornet allowed himself to enjoy the morning breeze and gentle sun and let the water wash up against his feet. He strolled down the beach to a small fishing village. The boats were already out; most were manned by loyal Hezbollah men. He was under close guard the entire time, though an outsider would not have been able to tell. One guard, the newest, a teenager named Yasser, cleaned the pool. Another tended the old lady's backyard garden. The Hornet took a small Koran out of his pajama pocket and read a few passages. When the Hornet was finished he walked back up to the villa, and before doing anything else, swam fifty laps in the pool. Then, and only then, and by the time he was finished the hour was approaching 0700, did the Hornet don a pair of khakis and a white shirt and go inside the villa to his headquarters.

He sat at the dining room table where a plate of fruit, prepared by the old woman, waited alongside several newspapers including the Lebanese *Daily Star*, but also the *Jerusalem Post* and *Harretz*, brought to him every morning by his longtime aide, Ali. Beneath these was a thick folder, containing military reports, dispatches, and on this morning a letter from Hezbollah's Secretary General. He was tempted to open and read but didn't. *Patience, always patience*, he reminded himself. Not until he had eaten his breakfast, leafed through the newspapers, and quickly gone over the reports did the Hornet open the letter from the supreme leader. It was one sentence:

Brother,

By the will of Allah, Peace Be Upon Him, I write this letter to you, my loyal comrade and friend in Jihad and Resistance, to deliver one message: Tonight.

The Hornet smiled.

TEL NOF

Operation Gideon Strike was over but Maccabee Force had yet to be disbanded. Having fired the first shots of the war, Maccabee Force would launch Israeli's counterattack in the next stage. More than 60 F-16s waited on the tarmac at Tel Nof, laser guided bombs under their wings, for General Peled to issue the order to scramble.

Peled was sitting at a desk in Tel Nof's operations center, located in an underground bunker, and waiting for the inevitable. The television in his temporary office was tuned to the BBC, which he watched absentmindedly. A news anchor talked with a pair of media 'experts' on the Middle East. One was a columnist from the *Times of London*, the other a researcher from a British think tank whose name Peled didn't care to remember. He was marveling at the magnificent depth of the ignorance of both panelists when the anchor interrupted them and said. 'I'm sorry to interrupt you both but I am getting word of breaking news…out of Berlin, where we will now go to live.…'

The screen went dark for a moment and then flashed to a new location. It showed a nighttime skyline of two and three story buildings. In the background, one of the buildings was a mass of smoldering steel, concrete and flame.

The reporter there on the ground, a young producer actually, identified himself and began talking. 'I am here in Berlin where apparently the Israeli embassy has exploded.'

'Has it…has it been attacked?' asked the anchor.

'I cannot say for sure, Martin. All I know is that about ten minutes ago, we all heard a massive explosion. It rattled the windows of my apartment.'

'You live close to the embassy there?'

'Yes, Martin, about four blocks, as it happens. I have walked past the Israeli embassy many times. It is, was, a beautiful old building. Judging by what I see here, it's gone, just gone, it's in flames…'

Before the Berlin producer could continue, he was interrupted by the anchor. 'Oh my god,' he said. Then, 'Hold on, we now go to Madrid, where the Israeli embassy there is engulfed in flames…'

The TV switched to a nearly identical image, this time showing a burning building in Madrid. A reporter and camera crew were on scene. 'About five minutes ago the city of Madrid was rocked by a massive explosion which has apparently destroyed the Israeli consulate here.' The camera showed the building, the front third blasted off, the rest in flames...

WASHINGTON, DC

Boddicker always felt most comfortable in his private study at home. A single man, he spent most of his evenings there. The room was a carefully crafted political testament, easily discernible to those who were paying attention. His library of more than 2000 books held all the classics of the ancient world. There were several shelves dedicated to British history, the great prime ministers, the empire, and Britain's slow decline after World War II. He had an entire wall dedicated to works about great diplomats like Metternich, Richelieu, soldier statesmen like John Marshall and even the ancient Athenian, Themistocles. Everything Henry Kissinger, a predecessor at the NSA, had ever written was on another shelf, as were memoirs by the likes of Warren Christopher, Zbigniew Brzezinski, and Condi Rice (the last two also predecessors at the NSA). You could always learn plenty from those who were always wrong, he once told a surprised guest. There was also the memoirs of James Baker- an autographed copy no less. Boddicker had always admired his ruthlessness.

On this night, before he retired to his personal gym, he sat in his study and proofread a memo he wanted the president to see. The memo was titled, *Hezbollah Intentions*. He read through the opening until he got to the meat of the memo:

> In any conflict with Israel, Hezbollah cannot possibly hope to win a conventional military engagement. Israeli forces are better trained and armed, and will be able to draw on air and artillery support as well as sophisticated real time intelligence data relayed by UAVs. Though they will suffer significant losses in men and material, more on this in a moment, the Israelis will do whatever they like in Lebanon. Hezbollah can't stop them.

So why then would Hezbollah fight at all? They will do so because they have a military strategy to achieve political ends. Hezbollah will inflict pain, pain on the Israelis and pain on the Lebanese.

Hezbollah's first goal is to inflict pain in the form of man and material losses. These can be reported to the outside world and portrayed as if Israel is losing. Hezbollah almost certainly hopes to drag out the conflict and inflict significant losses on the Israelis. As losses mount the internal clamor for an end to the war will mount as well.

A second aspect of Hezbollah's pain strategy is the Israeli home front. Hezbollah will no doubt shower Israel with rockets. Their targets will be Israeli civilians and infrastructure. While such attacks will no doubt embolden some Israelis to continue the war, Hezbollah hopes that by attacking civilians, they can convince Israel that the price of the war is too high.

Hezbollah will fight its war behind willing and unwilling civilian shields. Inevitably hundreds of civilians will be killed in the conflict. Hezbollah hopes to build international outrage and force the International Community to intervene on their behalf against Israel. Expect to see dozens of images of dead civilians being pulled from rubble, especially children.

The coming Israel/Hezbollah conflict will be a race to see if Hezbollah inflict enough pain upon Israel to force them to stop before the IDF's mission is accomplished.

Boddicker made a few minor corrections but otherwise agreed completely with the memo's assessment of the situation.

He was wondering whether to start with the treadmill or the exercise bike when the secure phone to the NSA rang. He knew it could mean only one thing.

Boddicker picked up the phone, 'Yes?'

'There's been a pair of horrible terrorist bombings against the Israeli embassies in Madrid and Berlin.'

'I thought they might try something like that,' said Boddicker. 'Anything else?'

'Satellites show, and human intelligence reports, lots of Hezbollah activity in southern Lebanon.'

JERUSALEM

'How did they get through?' Eitan asked as she stared at the list of Israeli dead and wounded at Madrid and Berlin. 'Wasn't there extra police protection?'

'Yes,' said Alon, 'but only a few police cars were blocking the streets. It appears the terrorists had two vehicles. One to ram through the block, the other to attack the embassies.'

'In both cases?'

'Yes.'

'Why Madrid? Why Berlin?'

'It is symbolic, Prime Minister,' said Alon. 'The scene of the Inquisition, Ferdinand and Isabella's expulsion of the Jews.'

'And Berlin,' said Eitan.

'Yes.'

She looked around at the cabinet. 'The question now, ladies and gentlemen, is our response.'

'Do we know for certain it was Iran?'

'They have not yet claimed responsibility.'

'Qods Force is fully capable of mounting an operation such as this,' said Sedor.

'General Ben Zvi, does this action by Iran preclude Operation Break their Bones?'

'Prime Minister, Operation Break their Bones can be executed regardless of Iranian action,' Sedor said. 'If I were Iran, I would not stop at this. They just endured a highly effective and humiliating attack. They will need to regain face in the Muslim world. I do not believe they would stop at a pair of embassy bombings.'

'Then what next?' asked Eitan.

'Something from Lebanon would be the obvious and easiest choice.'

There were more nods of agreement.

Eitan asked, 'General Ben Zvi?'

'Northern Command is on alert and ready. We are monitoring the border, and Maccabee Force can be in the air with an hour's notice.'

'And then we will strike them first,' said Eitan.

'Shall I release General Peled?' asked General Ben Zvi.

'Yes,' said Eitan. 'The order to attack is his to give.'

'And then the campaign falls to General Nagid.'

Later that night, Prime Minister Eitan took a glass of vodka in her private study. She looked to the wedding photo of her parents she kept on her desk and toasted them. As Russian immigrants, the Eitans- Paltrovksys in Russia- had drunk vodka prodigiously, but Eitan had never been able to acquire the taste. She drank it now though. She laughed a little and shook her head.

She ruminated until the phone rang.

'Yes.'

It was Minister Levi, 'Prime Minister, General Peled has given the go order.'

'Thank you,' Eitan said. She hung up the phone.

Her eyes fell to the map of northern Israel and then back to her parent's wedding photo.

'Well Mother and Father,' she began. 'You would love the general I appointed to head Northern Command.'

CHAPTER II

OPERATION
BREAK THEIR BONES

...bullets don't slam into Nagid, Nagid slams into bullets

...he once lost a firefight just to see what it felt like

...getting killed is against orders, and Nagid's men never disobey orders

...Sadat signed the peace accord because he was afraid that one day he'd have to fight Nagid

...Nagid was once bitten by a python, the python died

...alligators surrender rather than wrestle him

Israeli Military Forum Topic Thread: General Natan Nagid the Most Interesting and Deadly Man in the World

Nagid's Brigade annihilates Hamas Iranian Unit. 'No Prisoners' Vowed Nagid

The Jerusalem Post

Israeli General Natan Nagid Charged with War Crime in Brussels. Held gun behind prisoner's head and fired to coerce information

Times of London

NORTHERN ISRAEL

General Natan Nagid stood atop the engine deck of a Merkeva tank just a few hundred yards from the border. He scanned the hills with his binoculars and admired Hezbollah's handy work. Israeli intelligence knew for a fact that Hezbollah was moving missiles and launchers into place, yet he could see nothing.

'Still dark, General?' asked one of his aides, who stood on the ground next to the tank.

'Not for long.'

General Nagid waited another minute until he heard a sonic boom, and then another and another until it sounded like the sky itself was being attacked. Then the sky started to fill with strings of flares dropped by Israel jets, scores and then hundreds of them, each casting yellow light on the hills below. Five minutes into the noise and light show the Israeli side of the border came alive with a light show of its own, this time the light of artillery as dozens of batteries opened fire on known missile concentrations, confirmed bunkers and the hundred or so Hezbollah mobile launchers then being deployed.

'Let's go, Maccabee Force,' Nagid said.

Nagid saw an explosion at the base of a rocky hill a few miles inside the Lebanese border. He trained his glasses on the conflagration in time to see a Hezbollah rocket cartwheel into the air. There was another such explosion at the top of the hill as Israeli artillery caught another Hezbollah battery as it was setting up. As the minutes ticked past, Nagid counted seven more secondary explosions, all of which had to be rocket launchers or at least the vehicles transporting them. Sonic booms continued to shatter the sky and flares fell from it, but nothing else.

He scanned the line of hills with his binoculars one last time and said, 'Alright. I've seen enough.'

Nagid hopped down from the back of the Merkeva and started toward his track. 'Take me to the shore. I want to see if we can get a look at our coastal operations.'

'Yes, sir,' said the aide.

Like the rest of the north, here the beach was dark, but they could see a few Israeli flares and hear the sonic booms. He stepped out of his armored car and stared out into the Mediterranean until he saw them, briefly illuminated by a flare, a small fleet of Israeli ships, two corvettes, three missile boats, a half dozen patrol craft, and a pair of landing ships, all steaming north for the Lebanese coast.

EASTERN LEBANON

Aidasse is a small, pleasant town nestled between three hills on the western edge of the Metulla Salient. It is cursed because the main east-west highway in southern Lebanon begins there. For nearly an hour the town had been bombarded, first by sonic booms and flares, then by noise and flash bombs detonated in the streets and on the rooftops. At the end of that hour the people of Aidasse heard the approaching beat of helicopter rotors, each grew louder and more persistent and then peaked before fading away to the west. A minute later there was another wave of helicopters above. These too grew louder and then passed west down the main highway. The fourth wave grew closer, but rather than draw away to the west, hovered over the town and grew incredibly loud until the people huddled in their basements and cellars could not even hear themselves talk and it seemed as if a hundred helicopters were over Aidasse.

In a darkened Blackhawk cabin, Sgt. Rada Beta turned to his squad of Israeli paratroopers and said, 'We land in one minute! We secure the intersection and occupy the main building in the west fork. Then we shoot everything Hezbollah!'

The paratroopers nodded.

Beta turned his attention to the battle below. The rooftops seemed to explode as the dozens of Hezbollah fighters within the town brought the Israeli helicopters under fire. Door gunners in the Israeli Blackhawks returned fire targeting each rooftop until the enemy fire ceased. After the roof of the fourth building was left pock marked and smoking, the rest of the Hezbollah fighters on the rooftops of Aidasse kept their heads down.

Beta's Blackhawk swooped down and hovered a few feet over the streets. Beta jumped out; his men followed. Before him the road forked around a small two-story house. He ordered a four man section to either side of the road and led another inside the house. Beta kicked in the door and shouted in Arabic for everyone to stay down. He was greeted by AK-47 rounds fired clumsily by a Hezbollah fighter at the other end of the hallway. Beta hit the deck and returned fire, splitting the man in two with a quick burst from his rifle. He shouted again, this time a warning for civilians to identify themselves. When nobody did so he tossed a grenade into the room on his right. Pillows and broken furniture flew out the doorway. He threw another grenade into the room on his left, shredding several couches. Beta led the section down the entryway to the foot of the stairs. They took the second floor by storm, finding three Hezbollah men there. One stupidly fired an RPG, but Beta ducked out of the way and let it fly out the window behind him. He shot the fighter holding the RPG, while one of his section mates riddled the other two with bullets. One of them went down whimpering, 'Allah, Akbar.'

Beta and his section crept to the second floor windows and peered out. Their night vision goggles illuminated several Hezbollah fighters in the house across the street. Beta sent the other two men in his section to the roof, including the paratrooper with the Squad Automatic Weapon, and brought the home under fire. The two fighters on the roof were quickly gunned down by the SAW, but the two in the second floor window were still firing, and Beta didn't want to pepper the floor with MG fire in case there were civilians there. Beta shot one. When the other didn't show for two minutes, Beta figured he ran away.

With their position secured, Beta's men hunkered down and watched the fight within the town unfold. The rest of the battalion pushed west along the main boulevard, with one squad leapfrogging past the other. Hezbollah fighters soon abandoned the rooftops as Israeli paratroopers on the hills north and south of the town could spot them. They still fired from inside houses though, and the paratroopers had to stop and engage each target. It took the battalion two hours to get to the triangle in the center of town. Here Hezbollah was dug in, and Beta and his men watched as a barrage of anti-tank rockets streaked out of the clump of houses. At that point Apaches were called in to support the drive. Hezbollah fighters fired RPGs at them, but these streaked harmlessly into the night. Backed by the Apaches, the paratroopers advanced, taking the triangle house by house over the course of an hour.

The main body of paratroopers reached Beta's position just after 0300. Around that time Israeli jets could be seen attacking targets on the ground. Beta personally saw a pair of F-16s a few miles to the north dive and fire their nose cannons at a target and then peel away. Not long after he saw another pair of F-16s, this time to the south, hit one of the distant hills with laser guided bombs. There was a pair of explosions and then a large secondary blast.

'I wonder what took them so long?' one of his men asked.

Before Beta could answer, a flight of two Apaches roared overhead, one helicopter for each side of the road. Moments later the head of the column appeared in the center of the town and made its way west. A platoon of APCs passed Beta's position, then truck-mounted infantry. Then came the tanks and for the next several minutes Beta watched from the rooftop as Merkeva tanks rolled past. At 29 Merkevas they kept coming. He stopped counting and watched as they rolled deeper into Lebanon.

NORTH BEIRUT

After going through his morning prayers, meditation and swim, the Hornet sat at his villa's dining room table. He looked at the map of Lebanon and considered the military situation. On the coast an Israeli brigade had landed north of Tyre, a move that he had expected. But instead of occupying the city or pushing inland, the Jews had deployed a battalion at each of the road junctions on Tyre's outskirts. From these junctions a motorist could proceed north south or east, deeper into Lebanon. On the eastern border the Jews had taken the town of Aidasse and then pushed a significant force, probably a brigade, nearly ten miles west to Ghandouriye. To the Hornet's eye, this part of the Israeli plan made sense. They had cut off the two main arteries leading to the north (though there were plenty of back roads). He was surprised though, that the Jews had so far made no effort to secure the southern border to prevent Hezbollah from shelling northern Israel. The Hornet had been counting on this and more than 30 platoons, nearly 1000 men, were deployed along the border in anticipation. So far, nothing from the Jews, who seemed content to let Hezbollah mortar teams bombard the north of the country.

The Hornet was not pleased with the rocket war. He had been tricked by the Jews, he had to admit. Though they had filled the sky with aircraft during their opening bombardment, the Israelis had relied almost exclusively on artillery and used light and noise to simulate aerial attacks. When Israeli jets finally did strike, Hezbollah's rocket commanders had been totally unprepared. Nor had he anticipated their willingness to send helicopters against launchers concealed within private homes. Past history suggested the Israelis would not risk civilian casualties.

As the day progressed, the actions of the Jews, or more appropriately, inaction confused the Hornet, and they disappointed him. Israeli forces north of Tyre and outside Ghandouriye did not advance but remained in their positions. Another brigade had been landed outside of Tyre as well, but as with the effort in the east, the Zionists did not advance in the west. There was no fighting along the southern border, just heavy artillery shelling and aerial attacks on Hezbollah positions. To the Hornet's dismay every position the Jews attacked was a Hezbollah bunker or troop concentration. None of Hezbollah's efforts to conceal weapons among the civilian population had succeeded. In one case a Hezbollah platoon masked as a procession of Maronite nuns had been shelled by Israeli artillery. At noon a pair of mosques in the Beqaa Valley had been bombed and obliterated in spectacular explosions which revealed them to be ammunition depots.

The phone rang intermittently all day. Ali answered it and relayed the messages to the Hornet. These were always in the forms of questions, 'Should Green Group Four move to Sidon?' and so on. The Hornet simply nodded his head in assent or shook it in disapproval. He was too isolated from the battlefield, by the necessity of security, to micromanage and his commanders were expected to think and act on their own. His one standing order was 'march to the sound of the guns.- if you see Zionists, attack them.'

That evening the Hornet said his prayers outside beneath the setting sun. He was interrupted by Ali, who stood over his shoulder until he finished. The Hornet got up on his knees and said, 'Yes, Ali.'

'Commander Saladin says Jew helicopters are landing troops on the hills outside of Nabatieh.'

SOUTHERN LEBANON

The flight of Blackhawks came in low and fast over southern Lebanon. Had he bothered to look out the window, Gonzo would have seen Hezbollah rockets launching into the air, smoke plumes from destroyed rocket batteries and shattered buildings, and Israeli F-16s making strafing runs against Hezbollah positions. Instead, Gonzo was making edits to the copy he had just written about the Blackhawk flight's previous mission:

> Over the Skies of Lebanon: Our section of Blackhawk Helicopters came in fast over a small village somewhere south of the Litani. The Hezbollah fighters in the village did not see us, nor did they expect us. We were over the village just in time to see a salvo of rockets actually being launched from tubes inside of a small stucco house. The tubes stuck out of a first floor window where a normal house would have had a flower box. We saw the flash of light, then another and another. The pilot of the Blackhawk reported the sighting and asked permission to engage.
>
> 'Copy Black-One,' he said, 'We are engaging contact.'

Through his infrared goggles the pilot could see a pair of Hezbollah fighters on the house's flat roof. The port side door gunner, tethered to the Blackhawk's deck by a slender cord, leaned out the side of the chopper, pointed his MG forward and squeezed off several bursts.

'Keep at them,' ordered the pilot as calmly as if he were ordering a slice of pizza.

The door gunner fired off several more bursts.

'They're both down,' reported the pilot.

'Watch out,' said the co-pilot just as a line of tracers reached up from the ground and slammed into the Blackhawk's armor. One round bounced off the door gunner's MG and ricocheted off this reporter's helmet. The pilot banked hard to port, away from the tracers.

'Taking fire, taking fire,' said the still calm pilot. 'Anyone see him?' He waited a few seconds. The helicopter banked hard until the port side was almost parallel with the ground. This reporter could look out the port window and see flashes of light from Hezbollah Ak-47s. 'Yes…second house,' reported the pilot.

We leveled off in time to see a second chopper swoop down on the Hezbollah MG and pepper it with fire.

'That got him,' said the pilot. 'Going in on the rocket launcher now.'

Amid a flurry of small arms fire we went at the missile tube. The pilot took us in slowly and deliberately until we hovered above the house. We were parallel with the home's second floor and could see the tube sticking out the window. The door gunner leaned out and squeezed the trigger, only to lean back into the cabin. Several AK-47 rounds slammed into us.

'Damn it!" the door gunner shouted. 'One of those rounds hit my gun, the action is kaput.'

By then a half dozen Hezbollah fighters had taken us in their sights. The pilot accelerated and flew us outside the village. From there this reporter could see a third chopper, firing its wing-mounted machine guns at an unseen target.

'You're not going to let that missile launcher go?' asked the copilot.

'Shut up, Rafi,' replied the pilot. He turned around and shouted at the starboard side door gunner, 'Your MG work?'

The gunner responded by firing a burst into the night.

'We go back in then.'

We came in faster this time. Small arms fire bounced off the underbelly of the chopper. We approached the house from the opposite direction and hovered parallel to the tube again. The starboard side gunner leaned out even as AK-47 rounds filled the air and fired a long burst at the tube. Then he fired another.

'Again.' ordered the pilot.

The gunner fired again and again, until the pilot shouted, 'Alright, that tube is useless!' A burst of AK-47 fire bounced off the chopper's nose. 'We are leaving!'

We flew out of the village airspace low and fast. The quartet of choppers regrouped to the east and we returned to base just inside the Israeli border.

After we landed, this reporter inspected the Blackhawks. All were scarred by small arms fire, and ours had a trio of bullet holes in the aft fuselage. An hour later I spoke with the flight leader, I'll call him Lt. Yuri. He judged the mission a success. 'This chopper section destroyed two rocket launchers, a small caliber AA gun, and has eleven confirmed Hezbollah kills,' he told me. I asked Lt. Yuri about the risk of civilian casualties. He chastised me, 'What about the Israeli civilians being bombarded by Hezbollah rockets?' After that, he walked away.

Still, there is no getting around the fact that Lt. Yuri, and the entire IDF are worried about inflicting civilian casualties. The Blackhawk I rode in had twin machine guns and rocket launchers on each wing, yet they went unused. Instead the pilot took us incredibly close to the target house and ordered the door gunner to lean out and fire at point blank range. Later I asked the door gunner, 'Shulim' how he could account for civilians. 'Well, you'd have to be pretty stupid to stick your head out the window with us hovering right there. Civilians would run and hide with the racket we were making. Most Hezbo men wouldn't stand around either.' I asked him what he would do if he found a Hezbollah fighter amongst a group of civilians. 'Shoot carefully,' he said.

Gonzo considered whether to write more but decided not to. 'Shoot carefully' was a memorable way to end the story and would probably make it past the military censor. By the time he had finished, the quartet of helicopters had reached the vicinity of Nabatieh, a city of more than 100,000 located in central Lebanon. To the south of the city was a line of three hills, each roughly two miles apart and affording a good view of the surrounding countryside. Each of the Israeli Paratrooper Brigade's three battalions had been helicoptered onto these hills the previous night. Flying over the eastern most hill, occupied by the 890th Battalion, Gonzo could see trenches, barbed wire, and a pit filled with large caliber artillery pieces. The guns were firing south at a target Gonzo couldn't see.

The helicopters continued east until they approached Marjayoun, a large town at the head of the Beqaa Valley. Gonzo looked south, down the highway that led from Marjayoun which would eventually parallel the Israeli border. He could see dozens of flashes and dozens of smoke plumes. Gilden slapped his shoulder. 'Hey, you probably want to get in on that!' he shouted above the helicopter rotors.

'Can you get me there?!'

'Sure!' he smiled. 'But not until we land!'

BEIRUT

'At least they have not yet bombed Beirut,' said the prime minister of Lebanon.

Over the course of his more than two years in office, Prime Minister Gatari had struggled against the various factions within his own government, especially the Sunni/Hezbollah bloc, and had kept the peace. Now, from the balcony of his private home in Beirut - his security chief insisted he avoid the official residence - he watched his country being torn apart by war. The Israelis, he knew, would thoroughly smash Lebanese infrastructure, roads, bridges, the Beirut/ Damascus Highway would be cratered from one end of the country to the other. Judging by the fireballs in the sky to the south they had already attacked the airport. A successful business-man himself, Gatari knew that Hezbollah's presence in Lebanon was costing his country billions of dollars. He walked from his balcony, from where he had been watching the IAF throttle his country, to his living room, where the TV crew from al-Jazeera had finished setting up.

He sat in a chair before the camera and allowed the makeup artist to dab his face to make him look tan.

'We will be ready in 30 seconds, Prime Minister,' said the producer.

He was introduced by a news anchor who recapped the present situation and then announced his guest.

'We now go live to Beirut, where the Prime Minister of Lebanon, Amir Gatari, is with us. Prime Minister, what can you report on the status of Lebanon at this time?'

Gatari was blunt, 'We are under attack.'

'Can you tell us what kind of damage the Israelis have done to Lebanon?'

'The damage is already massive and going to get much worse. In the coming days Lebanese civilians will have no fuel, no electricity, and will have great trouble getting food. My people are now dying by the dozens, every hour.'

'What of the Lebanese Army?'

'Our armed forces are in no position to confront the Israelis. They are not built to do so. We are not the enemy of the Israelis. They have a dispute with Iran; they should fight Iran.'

'So you are saying that your country is caught in the middle.'

'I believe that is accurate.'

'So what is to be done?'

'I beg the international community, stop this. Make the Israelis stop. France and Britain, have you no heart? How can you watch what the Israelis are doing to my country? I ask the United States to use its influence with the Israelis, and make them stop. Or are the Jews in your country too powerful...?'

When the interview was over, Gatari went to his balcony overlooking the city and the sea.

'That should keep Hezbollah happy for a few days,' he said to himself.

NORTHERN ISRAEL

General Nagid usually slept about six hours a night. Because he felt it was absolutely essential to start each day with a sharp mind, it was important for him to begin the morning by catching up on the previous night's events. This included IDF action reports, but also the morning papers. Nagid was an educated and cultured man, and he was not one to ignore a good piece of writing, even if it was by a journalist. So it was with appreciation for the craft that he read Gonzo's report in *Haretz* for the second time.

Kyriat Shmona- For two days Hezbollah had been mocking Israel and the IDF with rocket and mortar fire from the town of Marjayoun, a mere five miles from the border. Today the IDF finally did something about it.

Ironically, this Christian town was about to be fought over by Jews and Muslims. Marjayoun is an ancient town, with roots going back to the Bible. It is a pleasant place of multistory homes and small shops, rising gently up a hilltop from which several surrounding villages, predominantly Muslim, are visible. This battle would be fought in the shadow of Mt. Hermon, several miles to the east.

The Battle of Marjayoun began just after sunrise. As it had throughout the first two days of the Lebanon Campaign, the IDF began the battle with a noise and light barrage. Once more Israeli Jets crisscrossed the sky at supersonic speed, shattering windows below and dropping flares into the streets of the town. Blackhawk and Apache helicopters soon followed. These engaged Hezbollah targets within the town. This reporter, from less than a kilometer away, saw one Apache pepper a two-story building with nose cannon fire, silencing the Hezbollah fighters within.

Hezbollah fighters would fire and run, fire and run, often using the sewers of the town to move between buildings. The Israeli helicopters played this game for more than an hour. Finally, at 0815 hours, the brigade commander gave the order to advance. The Rou de Marjayoun runs through the center of town. It is a wide, multilane boulevard. The main Israeli effort would advance along it. There are secondary roads on either side of the Rou de Marjayoun, and the brigade commander detailed several platoons to advance along these in conjunction with the main, battalion-sized force. They advanced out of Qiaala, a village about a kilometer southeast of Marjayoun, which the brigade had taken in sharp battle the day before.

At the edge of Marjayohn lies a line of two-story buildings and about a hundred yards behind these, are a series of L-shaped apartment complexes. It was here that the Israelis met the first serious resistance. This reporter was riding in an APC near the rear of the advancing column when the fighting began in earnest. The battalion took small arms, machine gun, and RPG fire from the buildings along the road. Two RPGs hit a Merkeva tank, knocking it off its treads and forcing the crew to bail out. The rest of the column halted and opened fire. The stucco and concrete façade of the buildings exploded as thousands of bullets impacted upon them. With the column halted, Hezbollah unleashed a mortar barrage from within Marjayoun and launched half a dozen Anti Tank Guided Missiles from the apartments behind the road. An Israeli APC exploded, but the tanks were unharmed as their Trophy anti-missile systems knocked down the ATGMs. The barrage continued for several minutes until the Apaches swooped in over the apartments and brought the missile crews under fire. When the battalion commander was satisfied that the missile crews and launchers had been destroyed, he ordered the advance to resume.

A hundred yards down the road the lead APC disappeared in an explosion of fire and dust. As two APCs pulled up beside the stricken vehicle the battalion continued to advance, taking fire from buildings along the road and also mortars within Marjayoun along the way. Another APC hit a mine, and a minute later a tank lost its right treads. Next, an APC detailed to move in and cover the stricken vehicles itself hit a mine. The trio of vehicles was brought under heavy small arms and machine gun fire. A platoon of tanks advanced cautiously, engaging Hezbollah fighters with .30 and .50 caliber MGs, but not with their main guns for fear of civilians.

The column halted for a time. Then an ominous rumble could be heard coming from the rear, it grew louder until a pair of massive D-9 Bulldozers took to the head of the column. Israeli soldiers clapped and cheered as they rolled past, giving the drivers a thumbs up and flashing the V- for victory sign. It is not hard to understand why. These are armored behemoths with reinforced plows, specially designed to detonate mines and improvised explosive devices.

Advancing side by side the D-9s did just that. They detonated dozens of mines and pipe bombs. A pair of tanks and APCs advanced behind them, laying down covering fire. Small arms fire bounced off their hulls, as did an occasional RPG. The accompanying Israeli gunners kept a sharp eye out for ATGMs and fired whenever one appeared in the distance. One missile got close to the left hand D-9, but it was brought down by a nearby Merkeva's Trophy system. The twin D-9s had advanced about 250 yards to a collection of houses. Here, Hezbollah got desperate. About a dozen fighters ran out of the houses, shouting 'Allah Akbar!' and firing their weapons into the air. These were just cover for suicide bombers who came out of the house behind them. The attack was futile, all the fighters were cut down on the side of the road, and two suicide bombers were detonated by Israeli gunners before they could get near the D-9s. The Israelis shot the houses to bits.

Before resuming the advance. one of the D-9 drivers got out of the cab of his bulldozer and shouted up at Marjayoun. Then he reached inside and pulled out the banner of Maccabbi Ashdod, his favorite basketball team and shouted, 'You will have to do better than that, Hezbos!'

Once more, Israeli soldiers cheered. The advance resumed behind the invincible bulldozers until they reached the base of Marjayoun proper. Beyond this point the ground rises more steeply into a complex town of narrow and asymmetrical streets. Israeli soldiers deployed from their APCs in a rough line outside the center of town and awaited the order to advance deeper into battle....

General Nagid set the newspaper aside and turned to his aide.

'I would like very much to meet this reporter,' he said.

'Why, General?'

'Any journalist with the balls to report from the front the real story of the IDF is worth my time.'

'Of course, sir.'

'Make it happen, I would like to meet him tomorrow.'

'May I ask, General, why so important to meet this person?'

Nagid smirked. 'Ghost writer.'

WASHINGTON D.C.

'Mr. President,' began Boddicker, 'After three days of fighting, this is what we believe the Israelis are doing.' Boddicker highlighted the map at the head of the situation room. He pressed a button and several blue icons appeared. 'The Israelis have landed two brigades, we think, at Tyre.'

'But they have not occupied the city,' said Stettler.

'That is correct, sir. Now, they have also occupied the town of Marjayoun, here, at the head of the Beqaa Valley, and another around the city of Nabatieh.'

'Again, not in the city.'

'No , sir. But we think the better part of a brigade has been landed on the hills to the south of Nabatieh. Now, further to the south, along the main highway running across southern Lebanon, they took the town of Adiesse on the border and then pushed west to Ghoudirye in the center. They set up a kill box.'

'Kill box?' Stettler asked.

'Yes, sir. Last night, they hit everything in that box. Details are still coming in, and the Israelis aren't telling us much, but we know they slammed Hezbollah targets from the air. It also looks like a heliborne unit dashed out from bases at Adiesse and Nabatieh and attacked several Hezbollah targets within the box. We all saw news reports on the aftermath.'

Stettler thought back to the Fox news report in which an Israeli PR officer showed a long row of Hezbollah bodies in a meadow, killed during a nighttime firefight with the Israelis. The report went on to show the local skyline, which was dotted with smoke plumes and fires.

'The Israelis claimed they killed 124 Hezbollah fighters.'

'A hundred and twenty four,' Davis said skeptically. 'Not a hundred and twenty three, not a hundred and twenty five. A hundred and twenty four.'

Boddicker laughed. 'I know, but they have a website up.'

'A website?' Stettler asked.

'Yes, Hezbollahbodycount.Il'

'Jesus Christ.'

'Let's go look at it.' Boddicker clicked a few buttons and brought up the website. There was a headshot of a dead Hezbollah fighter, 'Hassan Aziz' read a caption. The background wallpaper was made up of dozens of head shots of dead fighters.

'If you click the name,' said Boddicker. 'You get his rank. This one's a corporal, and you get his home address.'

'Now how do they know that?' Stettler asked.

'Hezbollah's Resistance Army is an army like any other. They have papers, dog tags,' said Boddicker.

'If someone did this to our guys we'd be going berserk,' said Davis.

'People are going berserk,' said Ambassador Benard. 'Last night at the UN I was accosted by the ambassador from Mali, Mali mind you, who demanded to know how we could support such a monstrous country.'

Boddicker waved his hand, 'Oh, Mali is upset.'

'Mock me all you want, Mr. Boddicker,' replied Benard, 'But Mali has a rotating seat on the Security Council and there will be resolutions at the UN this week. Mali will be able to vote on them. All of the resolutions will be highly condemnatory of Israel.'

Franks spoke. 'Mr. President, from a domestic political standpoint, it would be bad if these resolutions were adopted.'

'Will the resolutions pass?' asked Stettler.

'We can stop some, but not all, not without a veto,' said Benard. 'The day after tomorrow the French will bring a ceasefire resolution to the Security Council.'

'How long can you drag out the process?' Stettler asked.

'Till the end of the week, at most. But in the end, they will force a vote. The resolution will pass unless we veto.'

Boddicker nodded his head in agreement. 'They'll pass it, sir.'

'What are your instructions Mr. President?' asked Benard.

'I'm open to suggestions,' he replied.

NABATIEH

During the night Beta's company was helicoptered onto a ridge about a mile west of Adiesse. They had been met by Hezbollah fighters who mounted a short, though spirited, defense of the ridge. The company advanced north toward the town of Taibe, receiving sporadic fire as they went. They entered the town proper at 2300 hours and encountered stiff Hezbollah resistance. As they pushed deeper into town, Beta had been impressed by the sheer volume of RPG fire. Every few seconds, one was in the air. Every house, it seemed, had at least one RPG gunner within. The rooftops were also occupied by gunmen. Israeli helicopters flew into the battle and hammered the roofs with machine gun fire. Near dawn the fighting eased, only because Hezbollah pulled out to the west. As the sun rose Beta watched in satisfaction as a large group of gunmen, making their way west along the main road, were caught in a barrage fired by artillery pieces out of Nabatieh.

After sunup his squad manned a roadblock at the north edge of town. The road fell down the ridge into the Litani River. Two pickup trucks, both Hezbollah, burned a few hundred yards away. Beta was looking across the river valley at the smoke plumes beyond, when one of his men tapped his arm and pointed down the road at a trio of approaching white vehicles.

'Company.'

'UN,' said Beta.

The vehicles approached slowly. When they were 50 yards away Beta stepped forward and held up his hand. A uniformed man wearing the UN's blue beret stepped out. He walked slowly toward Beta, hands at his side. As he approached, Beta could make out his green, white, and orange flag patch-Irish Army. Instead of saluting the Irishman said, 'Lo, there. A black man.'

Beta laughed.

'Sgt. Tim O'Neill,' said the Irishmen. He saluted.

Beta returned the salute. There was a low rumbling sound, and then an explosion to the north. 'What can I do for you?'

'I would like to bring some ambulances into town for any civilian wounded.'

'We can let you in. But we have to inspect the ambulances first,' Beta said.

'Sure thing.'

Sgt. O'Neill waved to his comrades in the lead vehicle. The ambulances came up afterwards, and approached the roadblock one at a time. A team of four men, two covering, two inspecting, went through each ambulance. As they did so, O'Neill asked, 'I did not know there were blacks in Israel.'

Beta laughed. 'I'm an Ethiopian Jew.'

'Ethiopia?'

'Yes, there were a few hundred thousand of us. In the late 80s my family was evacuated from Ethiopia.'

'How the hell did you end up in Ethiopia?'

'My father told me we are the descendants of Solomon and the Queen of Sheba.'

'Oh…sure…' He cleared his throat. 'You like it in Israel?'

'I was born in Israel.'

The inspection team gave Beta thumbs up after finishing the last ambulance.

'Alright, go on through.'

'Thank you, Sergeant Beta.'

'You are welcome.'

The two saluted and then shook hands. The lead truck in the convoy drove up. 'O'Neill got on the passenger side running board. 'Ethiopian, huh? Who knew?'

He waved as the convoy proceeded into town.

Off to the south, Beta could make out a long line helicopters, at least a dozen, flying east along the border.

'Hey, what are they doing down there?' one of his men asked.

'I would say they are getting ready for the next attack.'

'Judging by the direction they are heading, that will not be around here.'

'No,' said Beta, 'somewhere else.'

BEIRUT

Prime Minister Gatari betrayed no emotion as the commander of the armed forces described the military situation in southern Lebanon.

'So far 612 Lebanese are confirmed killed in the fighting,' he said.

'How many are Hezbollah?' Gatari asked.

'As you know, Prime Minister, we do not make such distinctions.'

'I asked how many are Hezbollah.'

'More than 400. But most were Lebanese citizens.'

'And the others?' Gatari pounded his fist in the table. 'Where did they come from. Syria, Iran?'

'I do not know.'

'How many did you let into the country?'

The general held the prime minister's gaze but said nothing. Instead he went on to describe the army's rescue and security efforts. 'So far, we have maintained order,' he concluded.

'Very well,' Gatari said.

'Prime Minister, let me mobilize our forces in the Beqaa.'

'No.'

'We would be sending a message only, Prime Minister. We would be telling the Jews to stay out of the valley.'

'And giving them a tremendous target. Not to mention an excuse to go into the valley.'

'We have three brigades there. Our troops could fight….'

'I said no.'

The general angrily stood up, 'Do the Jews control you?!'

Gatari remained seated and calm. 'No more than the Syrians control you.'

The general took a deep breath, composed himself and saluted. 'If you will excuse me, Prime Minister--'

'Of course.'

After the general left, Gatari held his head in his hands. 'Those bastards,' he said. 'They're giving the Jews a reason to tear Lebanon apart again.'

NORTHERN ISRAEL

Gonzo and Gilden sat in the backseat of a civilian car as it drove down a dirt road toward General Nagid's mobile headquarters. On this morning he could be found on the northern border just outside of Shlomi.

'You must have really fucked up for Nagid to demand to see you,' Gilden said.

Gonzo shrugged, 'I write what I write. The military censor approved. If he doesn't like that, he can go fuck himself.'

'Tell him that, why don't you?' Gilden reached into his pocket and took out his small Torah and dropped it on Gonzo's lap.

'What's that for?'

'I'd start reading. When you meet with the general, God will be the only friend you have.'

'What about you?'

'My story is going to be that I tried to stop you, but you wouldn't see reason.'

'Coward.'

The car stopped. Before them was a small collection of military vehicles. Nagid was out in the open, on a radio phone. When he and Gilden got out, Nagid looked at them, smiled and hung up the phone. He walked toward Gonzo, arms open and said, 'Ah. Mr. Gould. So good of you to come.'

In the background, over Nagid's voice, they could hear a rolling artillery barrage, and further still, the sound of jets engines. Nagid offered his hand, Gonzo shook it. Gilden saluted.

'Sergeant Gilden, military liaison, sir.'

Nagid returned Gilden's salute.

'Mr. Gould, please come with me.'

Nagid waved and walked toward his command car. He opened the back door, Gonzo got in. Nagid got in after him. Nagid grabbed the morning edition of *Haaretz* and said, 'I would like to talk to you about the article you published.'

'General, the half that is in print cleared military censors, I did everything I was required to by law and journalism ethics.'

'Wait, wait, my boy,' Nagid held up his hand. 'I want to compliment you on this piece.'

'Compliment me?'

'Good lord, yes,' he smacked the paper with the back of his hand, 'I loved this part about the D-9 driver and his flag. I laughed when I read it.'

'You liked the story?'

'I loved it. We need more reporters like you.'

'Uh, General, you hate my paper.'

'I do.'

'You once referred to us as Israel's Palestinian Daily.'

'I did. That does not change the quality of your work. I want more of it.'

'More?'

'Yes. I want you in the field, with our ground troops.'

'I won't write propaganda, General.'

'Write like this,' he slapped the paper again, 'that is all I want.'

'But the military censors cut out half of that story.'

'They did?'

'Yes.'

'Do you still have it?'

Gonzo reached into his pocket and took out his Blackberry. He tapped it a few times until the deleted section of the story was on the screen. He handed the Blackberry to Nagid.

…The Israelis held the line there for more than an hour, trading fire with Hezbollah forces. When the brigade commander was satisfied that Hezbollah gunmen were pinned, he sent two mechanized companies down and then up a side road which led into Marjayoun from the east. This reporter accompanied the column.

Lit up is not too strong a term to describe what happened when we entered Marjayoun. We seemingly took fire from every house, every rooftop. The tank in front of the APC this reporter was riding in was hit by a pair of Molotov cocktails. The gasoline bombs started fires, but the tank would not be stopped. One tanker popped his hatch, took hold of the turret mounted machine gun, and let loose a long barrage. Bodies fell from the roof of a nearby house. The side road ended in a T near the center of town. The lead vehicles in the column brought the buildings in front of them under fire. They exploded in a hail of bullets, dust, chipped concrete and stucco. The barrage was topped off with a round from a Merkeva's main gun, which demolished one of the houses to our front. After that the column split, one company going west, one south. The west column was brought under heavy rocket and RPG fire, but most of the incoming ordnance was shot down by the tanks' Trophy system. Hezbollah resistance seemed to wilt before the mechanized onslaught. The rate of missile fire slackened, as did small arms fire, and by the time they reached the Orthodox Archbishop's residence at the west edge of town, the fighting here seemed to be over.

Down at the base of the town, Israeli troops and armored vehicles advanced as well. Hezbollah fighters were now caught in a pincer. The Israelis dealt with them severely throughout the night.

Dawn broke, Israeli soldiers tended to their wounded and gathered their dead, this reporter is able to say that less than ten Israelis were killed, testament to the training and sheer firepower these young men bring with them into every battle. At the time of the filing of this report, 54 Hezbollah bodies were lined up in the center of the town. The faces of each were being photographed. There were eleven prisoners, all wounded and dazed. At least a dozen private homes had been destroyed and as this reporter was getting ready to file this story, the mayor of Marjayoun, a Christian, came out of hiding and gave the assembled Israeli soldiers an earful. The brigade commander came up to talk to the mayor, who said the IDF was lucky that most of the civilians had fled the night the Lebanon Campaign began. There are no reliable numbers, yet, as to civilian casualties.....

Nagid looked up from the Blackberry. 'They censored this? Why?'

'The censor declined to give an answer,' Gilden offered.

'Idiots. Probably feared your reporting of the attack up the side road. As if Hezbollah wasn't prepared already…idiots.' Nagid cleared his throat. 'I will see that this is cleared.'

'Thank you, General,' Gonzo said.

'Now, my boy. I'm sure you are eager to get back out there.'

'Yes, General, I am.'

'Where would you like to go?

Gonzo's eyes went wide.

'I mean it. Where would you like to go?'

'Well, General, I imagine that there is some aspect of this war that you have not yet unleashed on Hezbollah. Could I be there when it happens?'

'Of course,' he replied. Then, 'Smart boy.'

NORTH BEIRUT

For the first time the Hornet was worried. The night before the Israelis had dashed across southern Lebanon, ignoring their own losses and cutting a path from Gourdiyieh to the coast. The battle had been one to behold, with an Israeli armor column advancing down the highway behind a rolling artillery barrage and a screen of attack helicopters. The hills along the advance had been set upon by jets and helicopters which blasted anything that moved. Even a single Hezbollah missile launch had been enough to call down a massive artillery barrage from the big base outside of Nabatieh. The Jews would not stop their advance, any vehicle destroyed or damaged was simply pushed to the side of the road.

At first the Hornet thought the Jews were going to repeat their previous tactics. When the column encountered its first village, a flight of helicopters landed Israeli paratroopers who cleared it ahead of the main advance. But at the next town, the column just fought its way down the main boulevard, leaving follow-on forces to deal with Hezbollah troops, who were left dangerously exposed by the first battle. Local commanders were completely baffled at the next town when the Jews again sent in heliborne troops ahead of the main advance. After that there was confusion in the ranks and in the local command, with leaders not knowing how to prepare for the next advance by the Jews. Within eight miles of the coast, Hezbollah resistance collapsed. There had been heavy fighting at Abassiye, about three miles inland and the Hornet was pleased by reports that more than two dozen Jews had been killed. But this came at the destruction of several Hezbollah platoons, in all cases down to the last man. After Abassiye, the Jew's advance had been essentially a victory march to the sea.

The Jews were acting out of character in other ways. The publishing of photos of dead fighters along with their names and addresses was macabre, especially for a western army like the IDF. The move seemed borrowed from the Hornet himself, who sent photos of dead Russian soldiers to their families when he was a commander in Chechnya. The Hornet did not understand why the Jews would do such a thing. Certainly the international outcry was not worth the collection of war trophies.

Most dismaying to the Hornet was the rocket campaign. The Jews had proved to be most adept at smoking out rocket launchers and destroying them, many before they even had a chance to launch. Of those that did launch, more than half were shot down by the Jews' Iron Dome system. The anti-missile system was far more effective than Hezbollah planners had initially thought. They had also believed, as had the Hornet, that it would be deployed to protect Haifa alone. Instead the system seemed present throughout the north and center of the country, leading the Hornet to believe the Jews had far more anti-missile batteries than they let on. The mortar teams had had some success though.

The Hornet looked at the map. *I have been surprised, I have been fooled. Shame on me*, he thought. *But I have surprises too…*

WASHINGTON DC

President Stettler trudged up the stairs to the residence and walked inside. He flopped down on the couch in front of the TV and reached for the remote control. To his irritation the TV was on CNN. Before he could actually absorb any news, he had had enough of that for one day, he switched the channel to ESPN. He was just in time to catch highlights of the Brewers getting annihilated in Chicago and whistled in awe at the homerun the Cubs' first basemen hit onto Waveland Avenue.

'Jesus,' he said. 'Did that ball have flight clearance?'

'What, Daddy?' the first daughter asked.

Stettler didn't realize Kelly was there. She hadn't turned around or anything, hadn't even looked up from her IPhone, on which she was furiously texting away. She sat in front of the computer, which showed a YouTube page with footage of soldiers firing at a hill. A few years before he would have asked Kelly what she was watching. But now he just said. 'C'mon Kelly, could you at least wear a long shirt when you put on tights?'

Without turning around she said, 'I've seen pictures of you and Mom in college,' she replied. 'You didn't mind when she dressed like this.'

'Well…uh….'

Kelly finished texting and finally turned around to face her father. 'I don't understand why those guys can't just leave those poor people alone.'

'Who?'

'The Israelis.'

'Oh god, not you too,' he said.

'What?!'

'I've listened all day to people bashing the Israelis.'

`Israel? God, Daddy, I was talking about those terrorists.'

Stettler raised his eyebrows. 'Oh.'

'I mean, how can they pay so much attention to one little country, with like, seven million people. I mean, get a life.'

'Well,' the president said, remarking more in her sudden interest in foreign affairs rather than her pro-Israel stance.

'I mean, my friend at school, Becky, she's been to Israel, like, a bunch of times, and says the people are really nice and it's almost just like here but with beaches and nice weather…and cute boys.'

'Well, I'm sure it is,' Stettler said without taking his eyes away from the Baseball Tonight broadcast. He didn't really hear Kelly when she said, 'I just wish I could help them out…'

He switched to the BBC which was rerunning its prime time news show.

'The Israeli's illegal war on Lebanon continues,' said the anchor.

Jeez this guy really has it in for Israel, Stettler thought.

The anchor threw the broadcast to a reporter in Beirut. 'Israeli forces have cut a swath of destruction across southern Lebanon and have essentially broken the region south of the Litani off from the rest of the country. Hezbollah forces south of the Litani are now seemingly trapped...'

The rest of the report held little that Stettler did not already know. He only half listened until the field reporter threw the segment back to the London anchor.

'We have a spokesmen for the Israeli government this evening. Major Ben-Joseph, thank you for joining us again,' said the BBC anchor.

'Not at all, Martin.'

'Major, perhaps you could explain to our viewers why the IDF has driven all the way across southern Lebanon to the sea.'

'Well, Martin, I am not really privy to our military's plans.'

'Still, Major, can you tell our audience why the IDF has cut Lebanon in two?'

'Martin, the war is not against Lebanon, it is against Iranian-backed Hezbollah--'

The BBC anchor interrupted, 'Can you tell us if the IDF will now attack Hezbollah forces cut off in southern Lebanon. Hezbollah spokesmen say they are dug in and prepared to fight to the last, and that Israel will be responsible for the destruction wrought there.'

'I'm sorry Martin, but if Hezbollah does not want to see destruction in southern Lebanon, then their forces there should surrender...'

Jesus, thought Stettler, *that sounds pretty goddman ominous.*

NABATIEH, LEBANON

Beta had not participated in the day's fighting, but he had an excellent view of it from Aidasse. Unlike the previous day's attacks, the final stage of Operation Break Their Bones began at dawn. Beta and his men clearly saw the dust plumes and artillery fires as elements of Division 36 advanced north along the Metulla salient. He and his men had watched small columns dart into a trio of Lebanese towns on the border: Markoba, Huola, and Qalat. Just like Beta's battalion had on the first night of the offensive, these were merely laying the ground work for follow-on Israeli forces. The flying columns exposed Hezbollah fighters, who after days of waiting, engaged the Israelis with everything they had. Once Hezbollah positions were outed, the Israeli troops called in air and helicopter strikes. At the same time one brigade of Division 36 crossed into Lebanon and advanced right up the border, one by one entering Lebanese towns from the south against much weakened Hezbollah resistance.

Further south, another brigade of Division 36 spent the morning encircling Bint Jbail, Hezbollah's center of operations in the south. As they watched, Beta and his men played a game they called 'guess the explosion' based on the premise that one could distinguish between a burning APC and a burning tank by the size of the blast; the latter's ammunition would cook off. They also observed Hezbollah rocket launches, counting two dozen by 1200 hours.

'Do you mean two dozen rockets, or two dozen individual launches?' asked the platoon lieutenant.

'Two dozen launches,' Beta replied.

Those launches were often followed by Israeli artillery, F-16s or chopper hunter killer teams. Beta and his men viewed plenty of secondary explosions as Israeli airpower struck, usually an indicator that they had found the launcher before it could escape.

'I hope those bastards are blown to hell,' one of Beta's men said.

'Hey look at that,' said another.

Beta turned his binoculars south toward where a large column of thick black smoke was rising.

'What's that?' asked one of the men.

'Looks like Bint Jbail to me,' said another.

'Yeah, that's Bint Jbail, alright,' Beta said.

They could see small and medium flashes of light, and through his glasses, Beta could make out missile and rocket trails. Several pairs of helicopters were over the outskirts of town. Beta watched in amazement as one was taken under fire, wobbled, and then crashed to the ground. Jets circled as well, and swept in and out of the battle, dropping five hundred and thousand pound laser guided bombs. They could not hear individual explosions and small arms fire, just one dull, but steady rumble, the sound of a bloody street fight ten miles away. The thick black cloud of smoke was joined by another, and then another and another. By 1700 hours it seemed as if the entire town was aflame.

CHAPTER III

OPERATION ELEVENTH PLAGUE

It is possible, in fact entirely likely, that a non-state actor engaged in a struggle to the death with a conventional military, upon realizing that it is losing the real war and the media war, will decide to take action to turn the tide of the media war.

Professor Annon Statch,

Digital Victory in Modern War

MK: Were you ready for Hezbollah dirty tricks?

General Ben Zvi: We understood that Hezbollah would commit war crimes and try to blame the IDF.

MK: What actions did you take to prevent them?

General Ben Zvi: What actions could we take?

Testimony of General Ben Zvi before the Knesset Commission on the Conduct of the war in Lebanon

JERUSALEM

Eitan began the War Cabinet meeting by asking, 'General Ben Zvi, what have we done to the enemy?'

'As of this morning, Prime Minister, we have confirmed 749 dead fighters.'

'How many do you think are dead beneath smoldering rubble?' Alon asked.

'There is no point in speculating, Minister, but it is safe to assume many hundreds more are as yet unaccounted for.'

In the distance an air raid siren blared, a constant feature of life in Israel since the war began. Eitan asked. 'How many missile launchers?'

'One hundred and seventy of all types. We've shot down hundreds more.'

'What is the state of our forces?' Eitan asked.

'One hundred and three dead, two hundred and forty seven wounded.'

'One hundred and three?' Alon asked.

'Yes,' replied Ben Zvi, irritated that he had to explain war to a civilian politician. 'When you fight an enemy, and when you fight to win, you incur losses.'

'Too many,' said Alon.

'They are all too many, Minister,' said Ben Zvi. 'Losses now prevent even heavier losses later.'

'Enough,' said Eitan. 'What are our losses at home?'

'Twenty eight civilians dead.'

Eitan closed her eyes in pain.

'I would remind you, Prime Minister,' said Levi, 'that that is less than what we lost in the Passover Massacre.' He cleared his throat. 'Netanya, Metulla, and Kiryat Shimona have all been heavily shelled by Hezbollah mortars, as has every small town along the border. In many cases Hezbollah gunmen fired on the towns from across the border. Security forces prevented an attempt by Hezbollah gunmen to attack the village of Avivim. Another such effort was mounted against Zarist. Hezbollah gunmen did cross the border but were intercepted by police. There are indications that Hezbollah forces assembled for several more attempted incursions, but these were broken up before the attacks were launched.'

'Missile strikes?' asked Eitan.

'As of this morning five hundred and sixty two missiles and rockets have struck Israel. Nineteen have landed within Haifa. If Hezbollah has missiles with longer range, we have not yet seen them.'

Eitan looked at Sedor.

'They have them.'

'Is it possible we already destroyed them?' Eitan asked.

'It is possible, but would be extremely lucky.'

'So those missiles lie in wait,' Eitan stated.

'Yes,' both Ben Zvi and Sedor replied.

'A warning,' stated the prime minister.

'Perhaps,' said Alon. 'Perhaps one which should be heeded.'

There were audible groans.

'Hear me out. We have badly hurt Hezbollah. It will take them years to rebuild. We have eliminated the threat of an Iranian nuclear weapon falling into their hands. The military has done its job. Now, internationally, we are a pariah. We are looking at massive boycotts, and inevitably the harassment of Israel citizens, possibly the arrest of Israeli officials travelling abroad. Now may be the time to declare victory.'

'He has a good point,' said Eitan. 'General?'

General Ben Zvi cleared his throat again. 'I agree with Minister Alon's analysis. We will of course carry out any orders issued by this body. Caution is always good. But I think it would be wise to understand that we will never, never have a better chance to destroy Hezbollah.'

'When would you need a decision?' Eitan asked.

'We are assembling forces for Operation Eleventh Plague now. I would ask you to decide by tomorrow.'

'Very well.' She looked at Sedor. 'What progress have you made in identifying Hezbollah leadership locations?'

'Very little, I am sorry to say,' replied Sedor. 'We have, however, eliminated several locations.'

'That should not be hard to do,' said a skeptical Alon.

Sedor ignored the foreign minister. 'We know they are not south of the Litani, of course. They are not in the Beqaa either.'

'At least south of the Beirut/Damascus Highway,' said Ben Zvi.

'We do not feel they are anywhere in the Beqaa, not even in Zahle, or Baalbek. Too risky.'

'Beirut, then?' asked Eitan.

'I do not believe they would risk that. We nearly killed the secretary general in 2006 because he began the war in Hezbollah's Beirut headquarters.'

'I see.'

'Now, we have almost totally compromised their wireless communications network. We believe they are aware of this. We have also tapped Lebanon's landlines.'

'Is Hezbollah using these?' asked Eitan.

'Very sparingly. Most messages are being carried by courier. We are cracking that network as well. Still, they must have a quick way to communicate in case of emergency; landlines are the most obvious and secure way. We've stumbled upon several that do not seem to be regular civilian lines and not government lines either. One, running out of Tripoli is encrypted. We are tracing this one now.'

'Why? Asked Eitan.

'It might lead to someone important.'

SAUDI ARABIA

'The King demands answers, Cousin,' said General Rafah.

'What did you tell him?' asked Prince Abdullah.

'I said we were experiencing logistical problems. I told him we suspected Zionist sabotage.'

'Oh, he must have loved that.'

'He did, Cousin.'

'Where is the wreckage from the Zionist aircraft?'

'It is stored in a hanger at King Khalid Military City. I have ordered one mechanized brigade there.'

'And the other brigades?'

'Concentrated at the other military cities.'

'All except for 1st Armored Brigade.'

'Yes, it is outside Riyadh now.'

'Good.'

'The king expects movement, Cousin. I am expected to begin deploying the army to the northwest no later than tomorrow morning.'

'Then it appears we are running out of time.'

'Yes.'

The prince thought for a moment. 'We need to contact Mossad, and tell them we shall move soon.'

'Yes.'

'But do not tell them when.'

'Yes.'

'In the meantime I will pay a visit to that hanger in King Khalid Military City.'

WASHINGTON DC

Boddicker briefed the president over breakfast.

'Overnight, Mr. President, Hezbollah really whacked the Israelis.'

Stettler sipped his coffee. 'What does that mean, exactly? How did they whack Israel?'

'Well, I'm not really sure where to begin. Off of Tyre, they sunk an Israeli *Saar* Class corvette.'

'How'd they manage that?'

'Not sure. But this morning Hezbollah announced that it possesses dozens of martyr submarines.'

'Martyr submarines?'

'Suicide subs. I think they're probably something similar to the human torpedoes the Japanese used in World War Two.'

'Wonderful.'

'The Israelis say they prevented another such attack.'

'Hezbollah also launched half a dozen drones.'

'They have drones?'

'It looks that way. Remember. They're Iran's proxy. The Iranians certainly have the capability.'

'Oh.'

'They flew extremely low and managed to avoid Israeli radar. Two hit a hangar at Ramat David, setting it afire. It looks like the other four missed. At the same time Hezbollah fired a barrage of new Fadjir-7 rockets. They just issued a press release announcing the new rocket's existence. Several were shot down, but three hit Tel Aviv. One slammed into an apartment building.'

'Good god, how many dead?'

'Eleven at last count. Twenty three wounded. Hezbollah claims they can hit the Israeli nuclear facility at Dimona.'

'Then why haven't they?'

'Mr. President, if say, Hugo Chavez, attacked an American nuclear reactor, what would you do?'

'I know what the American people would want me to do.'

'Exactly, sir,' said Boddicker, 'but it's still a threat the Israelis have to consider. At the moment Hezbollah is still firing on Tel Aviv. One hit a store on Ben Yehuda Street as I was coming here.'

'So what are the Israelis doing?'

'They have paused at the Litani River.'

'Are they done?'

'Possibly. But they spent the night consolidating their gains in the south, rooting out pockets of resistance, chasing down diehards, that sort of thing. If they're going to halt operations, the Litani would be the place to do it.'

'If they don't stop, where do they go next?'

'I suppose they could try to capture Hezbollah senior leadership, the secretary general, their military commander. They could also try to cut links with Syria, though their bombing campaign has badly damaged the Beirut/Damascus Highway. If the Israelis were to advance north, I would expect a drive up the coast on Beirut and another up the Beqaa Valley.'

'Didn't they do that before, in 1982?'

'Yes.'

'Wasn't that a disaster for them?

'Well, politically yes. It ruined both Begin and Sharon. They took a lot of heat internationally, and the Reagan Administration was furious. But militarily the Israelis accomplished their goals. They annihilated the

PLO in Lebanon, forced Yasser Arafat and the PLO hierarchy into exile in Tunisia, and defeated the Syrian army in the air and on the ground.'

'Do you think they'll try this again?'

'I have no idea, Mr. President. I believe, right now, Prime Minister Eitan is trying to decide if she's satisfied with what the IDF has accomplished, or does she want to finish the job and destroy Hezbollah once and for all?'

'What would you do?'

Boddicker smirked.

JERUSALEM

Eitan watched as the TV news reported the latest horror unleashed by Hezbollah.

'But how did they do it?' asked the news anchor.

The reporter stood on the beach. Behind him was the town of Nahariya, just a few miles from the Lebanese border. Several fires burned in the background. 'Nahariya police have not yet pieced all the details together, but they can say with certainty that the Hezbollah terrorists arrived here from the sea.'

'From the sea?'

'Yes. It looks like they were trained frogmen. Nahariya police have found wet suits and small motor rafts, several of them...'

They turned their attention to the TV as the news anchor spoke. 'Once again, to recap for those just joining us, overnight, Nahariya was subjected to a series of terrorists attacks that have claimed the lives of at least twenty two Israeli civilians and several police officers, who engaged the terrorists in a series of running gun battles. Can you recount the damage for our viewers?' the anchor asked the news reporter.

'Yes, the terrorists attacked and set fire to three gas stations. These soon exploded, causing tremendous damage. From there they worked their way down Nahariya's main street, shooting at and throwing hand grenades inside stores. A second group of terrorists launched mortar bombs at random targets throughout the town...'

'Have the terrorists been caught?'
'At least three are dead, and several are believed to be at large.'
'At large?' asked the anchor.
'Yes.'
Eitan turned off the television.
'Well,' said Alon, 'Even if you wanted to stop the offensive...'
'I know,' she replied. 'Get General Ben Zvi on the phone.'

LEBANON

The Beqaa Valley burned. Division 162 advanced on a two brigade front, with one brigade attacking and taking the town of Mashgara in the west, and another driving on Rachaya in the east. Israeli armored and mechanized columns were met by a fusillade of RPG and ATGM fire. Images of knocked out Israeli tanks were beamed all over the world. But Hezbollah paid a high price for these PR photo ops, with the units assigned to defend Mashagara and Rachaya all but destroyed in fierce fighting in the streets and alleys. With two brigades engaged in the south, the division's other two brigades leapfrogged ahead and pushed north. As they were advancing through small towns and open fields, Hezbollah resistance was futile. Units attacking the Israeli advance were exposed, and most were engaged and driven off by air and artillery assets before they could strike the Israeli columns.

Gonzo was with the 9th Battalion of the 401st Armored Brigade, east of Zahle. Long into the night he typed his story on his laptop and gave it one last edit before he submitted it to the military censor.

Zahle: This reporter is with the lead battalion of a famous armoured brigade, which today added another name to its list of battles.

The attack started just after dawn. We advanced north from the vicinity of Marjayoun into the Beqaa Valley in the footsteps of another brigade, which opened a path for us. As we followed the lead brigade's advance, we saw the bodies of dead Hezbollah fighters, burned out and overturned cars, and occasionally a wrecked IDF vehicle. Among the fields and hills, houses flew white flags. Jets and helicopters filled the skies above. We could hear fighting ahead of us, small arms and machine gun fire, artillery rounds impacting, Hezbollah missiles, and sometimes rockets streaking into the air for Israel. Our own aircraft were not shy about attacking ground targets and it seemed as if every few minutes some IAF jet was swooping down on the ground and attacking a Hezbollah position.

After noon we entered the town of Rachaya. As we drove down the main thoroughfare, it was evident that a major battle had taken place here. Actually that battle was still taking place as we could hear and see fighting down Rachaya's side streets. Houses and store fronts were riddled with bullets. The bodies of dead Hezbollah fighters lay in the streets. We saw more disabled Israeli vehicles, taken out at close range by Hezbollah RPGs. We pushed through the town and then branched west across the valley floor and then north.

We were in for a wild ride. Hezbollah fired anti-tank missiles at us at close range. Whenever this happened the battalion air liaison would relay the enemy positions, and a pair of helicopters would circle the area and search out the missile launcher. Occasionally we were attacked from the roadside by poorly armed and trained militia.

'It was pathetic really,' one soldier said. 'I mean, what chance did they have? What did they think they were going to accomplish?'

These were young Lebanese men, not even full-fledged members of the Hezbollah Resistance Army, being used as cannon fodder by Hezbollah. There were also several car bomb attempts, in which suicide squads would try to ram civilian vehicles into the column. By mid afternoon, any car moving or staying still was shot up as we approached.

One track commander said, 'I sat at my .50 caliber all day. I went through an entire drum of ammo, and then half of another. You'd shoot up a car, and it just kept rolling forward. I kept firing until I was sure everyone in it was dead.'

With all the fighting in towns and villages, and the civilian vehicles being used in these suicide attacks, I asked a platoon commander about the possibility of civilian casualties. 'The war in Lebanon has been going on for ten days. They know what's happening, and they needed to prepare. They need to stay out of our way…'

In this manner the brigade advanced deep into the Beqaa. The valley, of course, is no stranger to war. The Allies and Vichy French fought here during the Second World War. Most notoriously, the IDF battled Yasser Arafat's PLO, and later, the Syrian army in the Beqaa Valley in 1982. Events in the 1982 war spun out of control, with Ariel Sharon pushing the IDF deeper into Lebanon and picking a fight with the Syrian army. Ariel Sharon was particularly concerned with Syrian SAM batteries in the valley, In several days of fighting, the Israeli army, though bloodied, pushed the Syrians north and east, past the Beirut/Damascus highway. The Israeli army eventually entered Beirut, an event which led to a Christian militia massacring several hundred Palestinians as Israeli soldiers watched. Sharon was later found partially responsible for the Sabra Massacre and had to resign his post in disgrace. Independent militias are in Lebanon today. These include the Christian Lebanese Forces as well as well as many others.

This reporter was granted a brief interview with the brigade commander on the matter of Lebanese militias. IDF orders are clear. They are not to interact with any Lebanese militia in any way, though he says they are allowed to offer medical help if needed. His answer about militias was brief. But he did go on in great length about the Lebanese Army.

'We wish they would stand up,' he said. 'We wish they would stand up for their country. We would like nothing better than to help them.' The General became impassioned. 'Their country has been turned into a terrorist camp. These Hezbollah thugs control the government, not for Lebanon, but for Iran. Sometimes I don't know what the Lebanese Army is thinking.'

As of this writing, the Lebanese Army has mostly stayed in their bases. Some troops have assisted with cleanup and rescue efforts.

'We have encountered a few scattered Lebanese Army soldiers, here and there. But they weren't under arms, and we sent
them back to their base.'

I asked the general if he thought the Lebanese Army would
attack Hezbollah. He said he didn't think so. I asked him what
would happen if the Lebanese Army decided to attack the IDF.

He shrugged. 'Could happen,' he said. 'It would be suicide.'

Gonzo made a few more changes.

They were outside the town of Zahle, which was blacked out below
them. The entire battalion was parked in laager, a defensive square. The
tank crews were on alert and the camp was cold. Jet engines were a constant presence as they flew north for missions and then came back south.

'What do you suppose they're hitting?' Gonzo asked Gilden.

'What do I look like, a general?' he replied.

'Drop the Brooklyn Jew routine, would you?'

'I am what I am.'

To the north there was a flash of light, then an explosion, and then
a billowing cloud of orange fire.

'Wonder what they nailed,' said Gozno.

'Fuel tanker, something like that. Judging by the size and shape of
the explosion.'

'Oh.'

'You know you've been in the field long enough - you really should
be able to tell these things.'

'Thanks, Dad.'

There was more explosions. 'Shhhhh!' said Gilden.

To the north they heard rockets and missiles, the sky filled with
tracers.

'Haven't seen that before I---' Gonzo was cut off by another flash of
light, this time in the sky, and then another. Explosions followed a few
seconds later.

'I think they just got a couple of our jets.'

'You think?'

'I hope not.'

THE BEQAA VALLEY

Helicopters flew Beta's platoon northeast, low over the valley. They passed the hills around Zahle and kept going toward the Lebanon Mountains which marked the western edge of the Beqaa. Ahead, in a small river valley flowing northeast to southwest, he could see a few fires, smoke, and gun flashes.

'Here's what we know!' he shouted over the helicopter blades. 'Two of our F-16s went down in that valley ahead. Looks like they were brought down by Hezbollah shoulder fired SAMs. A pair of search and rescue teams went in after the pilots. They came under heavy fire when they got on the ground.'

'Ambush,' said one of his men.

'Yes. Standing orders are to never shy away from a fight. So we're going in to get our pilots, help our rescue team, and fight Hezbollah. The best way to get out of an ambush---'

'Is to charge right into it,' one his men finished.

'I see you get what we are up to.'

The men of Beta's squad rapped their knuckles on the floor of the chopper.

'We land on the western flank of our little enclave here, secure it, then spot and engage the Hezbo's. We call down fire, arty, choppers, and really let them have it.'

'Do we have our pilots yet?'

'That information has not been passed along to me.' He looked into the faces of each of his men. 'Questions.'

'So we see the enemy, and we shoot,' said one soldier.

'Yes.'

They flew into the valley under fire. A line of tracers reached out for their Blackhawk, but the pilot evaded and flew down to the valley floor and hovered a few feet off the ground.

'Go!' shouted the pilot.

'Follow me!' Beta jumped down to the ground. In moments the entire squad was out. The pilot flew the Blackhawk back into the night. Beta accounted for all of his men and arrayed them in a rough line. '2nd Squad down,' he reported to the platoon commander. He heard the other two squad leaders report the same. Before them was a low ridge, behind them was another. Beyond that was Zahle itself. Beta could see a flaming wreck about halfway up the ridge.

'That's one of the downed F-16s!' he shouted to his men.

He reported the crash site to his L-T who then gave him permission to advance toward the wreck. To their north a brisk firefight was underway. An Apache swooped in and pumped 30mm rounds into the ground. One of the Blackhawks joined the fusillade, both its door gunners fired as well.

Second Squad advanced up the ridge in sections. They got to the wreck without taking any fire. The pilot was not there and the seat was gone. 'We are at the wreck. Permission to continue up the ridge.'

'Granted,' replied the L-T.

The first section advanced. After a few steps a Hezbollah machine gun opened up. Beta saw one of his men go down in a heap. The others hit the deck and opened fire.

'Taking fire!' he shouted as a pair of mortar rounds landed to his front.

'Sending help,' replied the L-T.

One of the Blackhawks came in, ignoring the fire it was taking from the Hezbollah gunmen below, and lashed the ground with fire. Under cover of the Blackhawk, Beta ordered his men forward. As his sections advanced Beta made for the man he saw go down. He got to him, rolled him onto his back and saw he had been nearly torn in half by a machine gun burst.

'Damn it,' he said.

He left the paratrooper where he lay and ran to the lead section. They were no more than thirty meters from the top of the ridge. The Blackhawk remained above; its door gunners fired quick bursts at targets below.

'We're advancing,' Beta told the L-T. 'Tell that Blackhawk to hold fire.'

'Copy,' said the L-T.

'Let's go!' he shouted.

Second Squad took the top of the ridge at a run. The sound of Israeli M-4 rifles joined the battle as the paratroopers cut down the Hezbollah gunmen they found at the top of the ridge. They took more fire, this time from another machine gun. The paratroopers returned fire and lobbed grenades until the gun was taken out. Beta's men quickly fanned right and left and secured the ridge. They counted bodies.

'I got a dozen dead Hezbollah fighters up here, L-T.'

'Sergeant, look!' one of his men shouted.

He pointed down the other side of the ridge. Beta ran over and flipped on his night vision goggles. On the road below they saw several jeeps and a pair of APCs. One of the jeeps flew a Hezbollah flag. Fighters were on either side of the road. 'Everyone up here!' he shouted. The squad ran to Beta's position and lay down in the rocks and grass above the road.

'L-T, I have a bunch of Hezbollah vehicles down here.'

'Are you sure?'

'One of them has a Hezbollah flag.'

'Alright. I'm sending an Apache in after them.'

The Apache came in low and flew over the Hezbollah column. The men down there shouted and waved, Beta couldn't make out what they were shouting. No one fired until a pair of gunmen in the lead jeep opened fire on the chopper. The pilot brought his ship around and fired his nose cannon. Rockets followed. The road below was enveloped in fire and dust. Beta and his men aided their fire to the barrage and tossed grenades. When they were finished, one of the APCs was in flames, the other was turned over on its side. The jeeps were broken down wrecks. Men were still down there, those that were left waved their arms.

'I think they're surrendering,' Beta said.

'Come up here!' Beta shouted in Arabic.

Several men got up and began walking up the ridge. Those that could held their hands in the air, several were helped up by their comrades. Beta counted fourteen in all. When the first man got to the top of the ridge, one of the paratroopers screamed for him to get to the ground. He pounced on the man.

'What are you doing?!' the man shouted. 'What are you doing?!'

The other gunmen shouted as well. Beta heard one of them clearly. 'We're not Hezbollah! We're not Hezbollah!'

Another screamed, 'We're Lebanese army!'

NORTH BEIRUT

Ali said, 'The operation was a complete success.'
'And the pilots?' asked the Hornet.
'We have them.'
'Execute them.'

WASHINGTON DC

The men and women in the White House Situation Room watched Hezbollah's execution tape. The two Israeli pilots sat back to back, bound together and blind-folded. Behind them was the yellow Hezbollah flag pinned to a concrete wall. As he watched, Stettler had expected someone to behead them. Instead a masked Hezbollah terrorist read a brief statement in English, condemning the pilots to death for their crimes against the people of Lebanon. The statement took less than a minute to read. When the terrorist was done, two other masked men came forward, placed pistols at the heads of each pilot and pulled the triggers. Stettler thought several of the people in the room would become physically ill. Davis put a hand to his stomach. Benard turned pail. Boddicker just stared at the flat screen. His face betrayed no emotion, but Stettler noticed that his eyes seemed to pierce the screen. *That's hatred*, Stettler said to himself.

'Shall I play the video again, Mr. President?' the AV tech asked.

'Oh, God no,' Stettler waved his hand. The tech pressed a button and a map of Lebanon appeared on the screen. 'There's no need to dwell on this.'

There was silence.

'Mr. Boddicker?'

'Yes, excuse me. As of this morning, the Israelis have taken the Beqaa Valley north to the Beirut/Damascus Highway.'

'What have they done in the center of the country?' Davis asked.

'Nothing but air and artillery strikes.'

'Are the Israelis going to stop?' Stettler asked.

Boddicker shook his head, 'I don't know.'

Benard spoke. 'The more this goes on, the more trouble in the UN,' she said. 'We are facing what I would call extreme pressure from the Europeans. Right now, the British and the French are holding off the Arab and Muslim countries, but they are facing enormous pressure at home to oppose the Israelis - diplomatically of course. There will be new resolutions.'

'Wonderful,' said Stettler. 'What now?'

'The French will propose, in lieu of a Syrian effort, a resolution calling for a ceasefire.'

'How is that better than the Syrian resolution?' Stettler asked.

'The Syrians are demanding a ceasefire, a complete Israeli withdrawal, the establishment of a tribunal…'

'I see,' said Stettler.

'Mr. President, my British and French counterparts have informed me, that if we veto this effort, they will abandon their attempts at a moderate resolution and instead work with the Syrians.'

For the first time, Franks spoke. 'Mr. President, since you vetoed those resolutions your approval rating has gone up an average of six points in an amalgamation of PPP, Gallup, and of course the Rasmussen poll. Nothing says strong leadership like the veto pen.'

'Is that really a reason to veto these resolutions?' Benard asked.

'I'm merely doing my job, Ambassador,' Franks replied. 'Mr. President, your numbers are up among Jews, Christian conservatives, and defense hawks.'

'What if,' Stettler asked, 'the French and British put these ceasefire resolutions through, we don't veto them, and the Israelis ignore them?'

'Would they do that?' asked Davis.

'I would,' Boddicker said. 'The Serbs got bombarded by UN resolutions and did whatever the hell they wanted to Bosnia and Croatia.'

'Lovely,' said Benard. 'If that occurred, I suspect there would be further UN action. It would be hard for us to remain on the sidelines in that case. There would also be calls in Europe for some kind of peacekeeping force, maybe even economic sanctions against Israel.'

'That would place us in an impossible situation,' Stettler said. 'We can't allow that to happen. Ambassador Benard, work with the British and French on those resolutions. Make sure they are watered down as much as possible. Talk to them about some sort of anti-Hezbollah resolution as well.'

'Yes, sir.'

'Also, have Ambassador Silber meet with Eitan. He is to tell her that we can't put off the UN much longer, and if they want our diplomatic support, they will have to abide by UN resolutions.'

Boddicker grunted.

'Something wrong, Mr. Boddicker?' Stettler asked.

'No, sir, but---'

'Is there something you would like to say?"

'Well, Mr. President, I was just thinking that if the Israelis are stopped before they've finished the job, they'll have to do the job again, if you know what I mean.'

'You mean if we don't let them destroy Hezbollah now, they'll just end up fighting again in a few years.'

'Yes, sir.'

'You make a fair point.'

Benard was about to speak up, but Stettler wouldn't let her. 'Ambassador, delay the vote as long as you can. But when the vote on the resolution happens, we will not veto it. Hopefully that will give the Israelis enough time.'

JERUSALEM

General Ben Zvi reminded himself to be patient and said, 'We need a full accounting, General. Your men killed seventeen Lebanese soldiers.'

Though he was angry, General Nagid held his temper. 'I took the Beqaa Valley in two days, and all they want to know about is this incident with the Lebanese Army? That was their fault for being in a battle area. I've seen the first report. Those paratroopers were in the middle of a firefight and say they saw a Hezbollah flag in the column. This is a setup.'

'Of course it is,' General Ben Zvi replied.

'If you know it was a setup, why are you insisting my men account for their actions?'

'That is the game, General. The Arab League is now talking about sending troops to Lebanon, and the Europeans are screaming at us. Have you seen what's happening in Syria?'

'No, General, I have been too busy laying the groundwork for the next phase of the attack.'

'There was a massive demonstration in Damascus this morning. One hundred thousand people, all of them calling on the government to intervene to save Lebanon.'

'We have prepared for such a contingency, Chief.'

'I know, but I would rather not fight Syria right now.'

Nagid said nothing. Ben Zvi suspected that Northern Command's GOC would like nothing better than to finish off Hezbollah and then turn his guns on the Syrians.

'Have my orders been altered, Chief?'

'Not at this time. Note, the PM has not issued a go order.'

'Understood. Then if you do not mind---.'

'Yes, General, by all means, get back to work.'

Nagid hung up the phone and looked at his map. To the west, Divisions 90 and 35 were in central Lebanon, a kilometer south of the Beirut/Damascus Highway. On the coast, Division 91 was just south of Tyre, while Division 36 was just to the east. Two brigades of Division 162 were just south of the Beirut/Damascus Highway. Two others were further south. Elements of one had surrounded Jeb Jannine and another, Rachaya. Other units scoured the valley and were still engaging Hezbollah units in small firefights. The IDF was giving every indication that a major buildup was occurring in the Beqaa. On the map, a large blue arrow was behind Division 162. An aide had scribbled notes next to the line, they read 'engineers', 'helos', 'MPs', 'supplies'. Inside the blue line, in thick black marker, was written the word DECEPTION.

An hour later, General Ben Zvi briefed the cabinet.

'There is no doubt, Prime Minister, that we have hurt Hezbollah,' he said.

'How badly?' Alon asked.

Ben Zvi reached into his briefcase and took out a manila folder, three inches thick. 'Inside that folder are photographs of every dead Hezbollah body in our possession.'

'That's macabre,' said Shoal. 'This apparent trophy taking is beneath us.'

'How many?' asked Eitan.

'In this folder are 932 photographs. General Nagid sent it down to me this morning.'

'What else have we done to them?' asked Eitan.

'Four hundred and thirty nine bunkers occupied. At least one hundred and twelve identified and destroyed further north. Three hundred and twelve launchers destroyed.'

'Then why are the missiles still coming?' demanded Shoal. 'While the military is reveling in the damage inflicted on Hezbollah, Hezbollah is inflicting great harm upon us.'

Levi said, 'One thousand seventy six confirmed rocket strikes. Thirty-eight civilians dead. That is on top of the thirty-nine people killed in the terror attack on Nahariya.'

'And the forty three Israelis killed in Madrid and Berlin,' added Shoal. 'And this horrible snuff video. How many more of those will we see?'

Eitan took a deep breath. 'General Ben Zvi, what are our military losses?'

'Two hundred ninety eighty dead, four hundred seventeen wounded. A further seventeen dead sailors. One ship sunk, twenty four tanks destroyed, twenty one tracks destroyed, two jets shot down, two helicopters shot down.'

'Why the emphasis on equipment?' asked Shoal.

'Every vehicle lost is a PR victory for Hezbollah.'

'This entire war is a PR victory for Hezbollah,' replied the interior minister. 'The more we fight, the more they gain.'

'They gain nothing if we destroy them,' said Alon.

'Can we do that?' asked Shoal. 'Can we really destroy Hezbollah?'

'We damaged their infrastructure. We have hurt their army,' said Alon.

Shoal looked to Sedor, 'How many members of their senior leadership have we captured?' the interior minister demanded. 'How many senior military commanders?'

'None,' answered Sedor.

'And can you guarantee that we will capture any of them?' Shoal demanded.

'Of course not.'

'Then I say we stop now.' The interior minister looked at Eitan. 'Prime Minister, you should put this to a cabinet vote, for the record.'

Alon stood in anger. 'Stop it right now. You cannot demand a cabinet vote. You should be respectful.'

'Sit down, Alon,' said Eitan. 'There will be no cabinet vote.'

'But---' began Shoal.

'The decision will be mine and mine alone.'

'What is your decision, Prime Minister?' the interior minister asked.

Eitan ignored him. 'General Ben Zvi, how long does General Nagid need to execute the final phase of the plan?'

General Ben Zvi would not let himself get pinned down to specifics. 'I would not dare put a specific time table on the operation, Prime Minister. There are far too many variables.'

'Well put, General,' said Eitan in admiration of Ben Zvi's studied evasiveness. She then got serious. 'I am meeting with the American ambassador in a few hours. He will most likely tell me that his government can delay a UN ceasefire resolution for only so long and that they will expect us to abide by it.'

'Prime Minister, how many days do you expect until a vote?' asked Ben Zvi.

'We think two, maybe three,' replied Eitan. Alon nodded.

'That should be enough time.'

'If we stop now,' Eitan said, 'we have done tremendous damage to the enemy, have we not, General Ben Zvi?' Ben Zvi nodded. 'Minister Alon?' He nodded as well. She looked around the table. 'Is there anyone in this room who does not believe we have badly hurt Hezbollah?'

Everyone agreed.

'Our standing in the world has been hurt much worse,' said Shoal. 'The pain we have felt at home.'

At that point the ministers began shouting at one another. An amused General Ben Zvi watched as Alon and Shoal took turns calling each other names. He then turned his eyes to the prime minister, who did nothing to stop them. *What is she playing at?* He asked himself. She finally pounded the table. Everyone went quiet.

'When I meet Ambassador Silber, I intend to tell him what course of action we will take. I will have my decision by then.' She turned to

General Ben Zvi. 'General, before I make my decision, is there anything else you think I should know?'

'Well…' he gathered his thoughts. 'If you are going for victory, if you want to be able to tell the nation and the world that we won this war, you have to be able to prove it.'

'How so?' asked the prime minister.

'Hezbollah must know it lost. The world must see that Hezbollah has lost. There can be no doubt. There can be no manipulation. Hezbollah cannot be able to say that they survived our onslaught. Even if the organization survives, it must be so badly damaged that no one will be able to say they did not lose.'

'How?' demanded Shoal.

'I would say, if this were a prize fight, Hezbollah would have to be bloodied, cut with a swollen eye, and stumbling.'

'Can we do that to Hezbollah? Asked Eitan.

'General Nagid thinks he can.'

Eitan excused herself and retired to her office. She sat at her desk for a few minutes and reached a decision. She then took out a piece of paper and wrote out a few quick notes. When she was finished she asked her secretary to summon General Ben Zvi. He arrived a few minutes later.

'I was just speaking with General Nagid,' he said. 'He reports that he is ready if you are.'

'Good,' said Eitan. She handed Ben Zvi the piece of paper on which she had made her notes. Ben Zvi read:

Conditions for Operation Big Cedars
1. No IDF prisoners left behind
2. Members of Hezbollah leadership killed or captured.
3. Clear, visual evidence of Hezbollah defeat.
   What are these, Prime Minister?' he asked. 'Goals?'
' Orders.'

CHAPTER IV

OPERATION BIG CEDARS

General Ben Zvi: We always planned a three stage operation in Lebanon. Each stage was independent of the other, so that should the national leadership decide to advance to the Litani, the IDF could do so without committing to operations north of the Litani or in the Beqaa Valley.

MK: Did the IDF's plans for Operation Big Cedars include engaging the Lebanese Army?

General Ben Zvi: We did have plans for such a contingency.

MK: So you planned to engage the Lebanese Army?

General Ben Zvi: No, that is not what I said.

MK: Then what did you say, General?

General Ben Zvi: We were prepared to fight the Lebanese Army if need be.

MK: But you did not actively seek to do so.

General Ben Zvi: No.

MK: Now, as to the Syrians....

Testimony of General Ben Zvi before the

Knesset Commission on the Conduct

of the War in Lebanon

MK: General Nagid, was an operation Little Cedars ever planned.

General Nagid: What do you mean, Minister?

MK: Was there ever planned, a smaller operation in northern Lebanon?

General Nagid: Not by me. Not to my knowledge.

MK: Why not, General?

General Nagid: What would be the point? I do not believe in half measures. Go big, or not at all.

Testimony of General Nagid before the

Knesset Commission on the Conduct

of the War in Lebanon

WASHINGTON D.C.

In the Situation Room, President Stettler watched in horror as the Prime Minister of Lebanon broke down in tears on TV. Gatari slumped to his desk and held his face in his hands, sniffled and then dabbed his eyes with a handkerchief.

'The world will forgive me,' said Prime Minister Gatari, 'But I weep for my country. I weep for a world that will not intervene to stop Lebanon's destruction. As I speak to you, Israeli troops occupy

144

southern Lebanon. They sit in the Beqaa, now, as the world watches. They advance up the coast, past Sidon, past Tyre. The Israelis are cutting the heart out of Lebanon.'

Stettler turned to Boddicker, 'But not coming down out of the Beqaa?'

'Apparently not,' said Boddicker.

'Because I have done all I can, as prime minister of my beloved, beautiful country, and because I can do no more, I, with great reluctance, resign the office of Prime Minister and dissolve the government....'

'Oh shit!' said Stettler.

'I think that's about right, Mr. President,' Boddicker replied.

NORTH BEIRUT

The Hornet's telephone would not stop ringing as the crisis unfolded. He was being badly beaten, and he knew it. Hezbollah forces were deployed east, opposite the Beqaa, to meet a threat that never materialized. Throughout the night the Jews advanced along the coast and through central Lebanon. The Hezbollah units deployed south, approximately 700 men, acted as little more than a speed bump, as the Jews attacked, supported by massive artillery and air barrages. By dawn the Jews had brigades in Jezzine where two Hezbollah units were waging a fanatical and suicidal last-ditch defense. Reports indicated that even as the battle of Jezzine raged, a Jewish brigade advanced around the town and pushed north. The Jews had had similar success on the coast road and then branched out east toward Beiteddine, where they no doubt intended to link up with the central column. Once they linked up, and the Hornet had no doubt that they would, the Jews would be in a position to drive on the Aley Ridge, the Beirut/Damascus Highway to the north, and then Beirut proper. Several Hezbollah units had taken refuge within the southern Palestinian refugee camps, but they had been harried along the way by enemy aircraft and casualties had been heavy. In order to slow the Jews' advance, the Hornet had tried to withdraw four of his best units, all armed with ATGMs and RPGs, from the Beqaa, but these had been spotted and all but destroyed from the air. One unit had even run into an Israeli company inserted by helicopters along the road leading from the highway south to Beiteddine.

As the telephone rang the Hornet read a handwritten note from the secretary general, brought to him that morning with a delivery of fruit and vegetables for the old women. The note itself astonished the Hornet. The secretary general's handwriting was scratchy and seemed panicked. He wanted answers. He demanded to know how the Hornet had been so badly fooled. It was most unlike the normally calm and patient Secretary General, whose confidence looked to have been shattered.

Just after his aide hung up, the phone rang again. Ali seemed astonished at what he was being told. When he hung up, he walked over to the dining room and said, 'Jewish troops have taken the airport.'

'Which unit?'

'Their Paratroopers Brigade.'

'Is the report accurate?' the Hornet asked. 'They were supposed to be outside of Tyre.'

'I believe so, the man relaying it to me is most reliable.'

'I see.'

If they are at the airport, he thought, *they are getting ready to make a move on Beirut.*

A few minutes later the phone rang again. This time the aide said, 'al-Jazeera is reporting that Jew helicopters are landing in Beirut.'

Everything the Jews had done until that moment indicated they would not occupy a major urban area. But now they were occupying Beirut. *I have been fooled once again.*

'We have twenty six platoons in Beirut,' said Ali. 'Almost a thousand men.'

'Yes.'

'They are moving to engage.'

'Good.'

I have lost the military aspect of this war, the Hornet thought in resignation. *But we can still win the media war.*

'Contact General Hassan. Tell him to execute Operation Beqaa Flag.'

NORTHERN ISRAEL

As his commanders were too busy defeating Hezbollah to send him accurate intelligence, General Nagid watched al-Jazeera to get a feel for what was happening at the Beirut airport. He was pleased. The anchor, from his desk in Qatar, could barely hold his outrage in check.

'Sami, please tell the world, once again, what you witnessed this morning at the Beirut airport.'

'As dawn broke, Israeli jets swooped in low over the airport and bombed the hangers here. Within minutes there were massive fires blanketing the sky. I can report that most of the aircraft in the Lebanese national airline inventory are destroyed. As the fires raged dozens of helicopters landed on the tarmac and disgorged hundreds of Israeli paratroopers. They fanned out across the airport and engaged any-one in uniform and carrying a gun. I counted at least seventy bodies.'

'What of the survivors? What of the civilian workers there?'

'Survivors and civilians were rounded up and are being held in the terminal. The Israelis have forbidden us from showing you the termi-nal or the airport, but I can tell you it is ringed with soldiers. Civilians were thrown to the ground by armed Israeli soldiers and handcuffed. They were then herded inside the terminal.'

'What of the Lebanese Army? Were Lebanese soldiers not there?'

'They ran away.'

'Please say that again, Sami.'

'They ran away, leaving their tanks and armored vehicles to the Israelis.'

'Did they not want to fight, given the Israeli massacre of their com-rades a few days before in the Beqaa?'

'Apparently not.'

'And the UN?'

'UN soldiers here earlier tried to negotiate a quick ceasefire to evacuate civilians, care for the wounded and see to the dead, but the Israelis would not allow it.'

'Sami, as you know the Israelis have imposed a media blackout in Beirut itself. Can you tell us anything about what is happening there?'

'At this point it is hard to know, but we have heard fighting.'

'Describe what you heard so the world will know, please.'

'Gun fire, artillery fire, and of course, Israeli jets. I cannot show pictures of Beirut. Just off camera is an Israeli military officer forbidding me to do so.'The reporter took a deep breath,'Hezbollah should know that just off the coast I saw several Israeli ships and they were...'

Before Sami could finish, an Israeli soldier stepped into view and knocked the camera to the ground.

Nagid laughed and turned off the TV.

'General,' said one of his aides.

'Yes?'

'General Peled has beamed to you some very interesting footage taken from a drone. He says you should see it right away.'

Nagid motioned to the flat screen.'Put it on.'

The aide ran a cable from his Blackberry to the flat screen. A black and white image of Beirut came on the screen. The operator zoomed in to show a walled compound. Nagid knew it well. It was the Iranian Embassy in Beirut. Out of the gate came several cars. Their security was horrible because Nagid could clearly see AK-47 rifles hanging out the windows. There was even a masked gunmen hanging onto the running board of an SUV.

'They must really be panicked to allow a security lapse like that.'

'I would think so, General.'

'Is Flotilla 13 still at sea?'

'On alert and awaiting orders, sir.'

'Good. Activate them.'

Nagid sat back in his chair as the aide relayed the order to Israel's elite naval commando unit. 'Oh how the world will hate this.' Nagid smiled.

BEIRUT

As head of the Lebanese armed forces, General Hassan had at his disposal eleven mechanized brigades, three specialized regiments, and five Interventions Regiments. Aside from regular law and order exercises in Lebanon's major cities, these had remained idle since the war began. The commanding general was technically neutral in Lebanon's great ethno-religious conflict. He was of a Sunni mother but a French father, who in turn was half Shia on his mother's side. He was known to have ties to the Amal Party, which of course was allied with Hezbollah and Syria.

He had not seen ex-prime minister Gatari. Even if he had time, he did not care to. Since Gatari's resignation twelve hours before, Hassan had been inundated with panicked calls from regional, brigade, and regimental commanders, all asking for orders. There was no one to issue orders. Since the resignation, the various sectarian political parties had been frantically negotiating, but so far no deal to form a government seemed reachable. So as Lebanon was torn to pieces again by the IDF, the nation had no government.

The Lebanese army was in a bad state. Three brigades in the south were bottled up inside their barracks. Two more were blockading Palestinian refugee camps, one in the north, outside Tripoli, another in the south along the coast road. Another three were dealing with refugees and providing security in the north, which had been relatively untouched by the war.

That left three brigades, two around Mt. Lebanon and one in the Beqaa. All three were in an excellent position to move south and led by officers, down to the battalion level, personally loyal to Hassan. Over the years the ranks of each brigade had been filled out with Amal and Hezbollah men until their numbers accounted for about half of each unit's manpower. On his orders, Hezbollah men had already tricked the Israelis into the Lebanese Army massacre at Nabatieh.

In his office at Army headquarters in Beirut, Hassan spoke to all three brigade commanders via speaker phone. All three generals reported their brigades were mobilizing. He asked about the reliability of the rank and file, each general thought that 90% of each of their brigades could be counted on.

'Even the men who are not Amal or Hezbollah are eager to fight, General.'

Another commander agreed, 'Yes, they see what the Zionists are doing to Lebanon.'

'They will be martyrs,' said General Hassan.

NORTHERN ISRAEL

'This is serious?' General Nagid asked.

'Yes,' replied the GOC of Division 162. 'Three Lebanese Army brigades are leaving their bases and moving toward our position. I can have drone images sent to you right away, sir.'

'Please do. Have you contacted the Lebanese brigades?'

'They do not respond.'

'How long before they make contact?'

'One brigade, the 8th out of the north Beqaa will be encountering the lead elements of 401 Brigade within the hour. Two others are moving south right behind.'

'Alright. I've got to update the chief.'

'What do I do, General?'

'What do you mean, what do you do? Order the Lebanese to pull back and if they don't engage them.'

'I would like that in writing, sir.'

'You shall have it.'

Nagid ordered an aide to write up the appropriate order while another got General Ben Zvi on the line. After Nagid informed the chief, Ben Zvi asked, 'And what orders have you issued?'

'I told Division 162 to stand its ground and fight.'

'Of course you did.'

'Do you support me, Chief? I can resign. Shall we say for mental health reasons?'

'Calm down, General Nagid.'

'Chief, do I have your support?'

'Yes.'

'You will clear this with the PM?'

'What choice do I have?'

'What would you have done, Chief?'

'The same.'

'I am glad to hear that,' replied Nagid. 'Oh, and one more thing, so you are not surprised by this, I think you should know about a little operation I ordered….'

THE BEQAA VALLEY

Gonzo was in the brigade commander's CP when the call came. A battalion commander reported that one of his recon platoons had spotted Lebanese Army vehicles moving toward his position south from the Beirut/Damascus Highway and advancing in combat echelon. The brigade commander reported it to division, who responded that they were aware of the Lebanese Army movement.

'What do I do, sir?' asked the battalion commander.

'Prepare to engage, but do not fire without my authorization. We are trying to ascertain their intentions.'

'The Lebanese intentions look clear from my position, sir.'

'Understood. Do not fire without authorization.'

The brigade GOC was too busy to talk, but Gonzo wrote down everything he heard. Then he and Gilden left the CP and went forward several hundred yards to the brigade's perimeter. Here a mechanized battalion was deployed among the parched grass of the valley. Two mechanized companies forward, with a third mechanized company and a company of Merkeva tanks deployed to the rear. Before them the ground sloped gently away to the north. A mile beyond was a small village and past that, the Beirut/Damascus Highway. Another mechanized battalion was on the right flank. By the time Gonzo got there, the men on the line were already commenting on the dust clouds generated by Lebanese armored vehicles.

'You think the Lebanese army will attack?' he asked Gilden.

Gilden shrugged. 'Eh.'

'C'mon,' said an annoyed Gonzo.

'Well, we are tearing their country apart.'

A quartet of F-15s flew overhead toward the Lebanese Army brigade.

'This is going to be very bad,' said Gonzo.

'Thank the Lord we have journalists like you to perceive these things.'

Gilden walked over to the nearest Merkeva. The tank commander was standing in his cupola, loading an ammo belt into his .50 caliber. 'Hey, Sergeant, you mind if we stand on your tank?'

'Sure. You will have to get off if we move.'

'Deal.'

Gilden climbed onto the Merkeva's engine deck and helped Gonzo up.

'We'll get a better view from up here.'

When it was all over a few hours later, and the ground before him was littered with burning vehicles and dead Lebanese soldiers, Gonzo filed his report.

The Beqaa Valley- The men of this mechanized battalion asked themselves and eachother the same questions, 'Are they coming?', 'Do you think they will attack?', 'What do we do?'

The Lebanese Army never attacked, not really, but the men of the IDF did their jobs.

As the Lebanese Army advanced toward IDF positions, the battalion commander tried frantically to contact his counterpart on the other side of the line but to no avail. It is known that the division commander tried to establish a link with the Lebanese army as well. IAF jets even flew low, buzzing the Lebanese as they closed in.

The Lebanese weren't stopping.

Much to the consternation of track and tank crews, the word came down from the battalion commander that they were absolutely forbidden to fire until the Lebanese fired first, or closed to within a thousand yards. The men grumbled, but followed orders. In desperation some tankers stood atop their vehicles and waved their arms in the air. Others turned on loudspeakers and pleaded with the Lebanese to stop.

The Lebanese soldiers weren't listening.

At a thousand yards the Lebanese opened fire. Their gunnery was wildly undisciplined, inaccurate and slow. 'At no time did I fear the Lebanese,' said one tank commander. 'Their shells landed to our front, and to our rear. They couldn't hit anything.'

The IDF unleashed a torrent of missile and machine gun fire. A second later the ground to our front was broken by a half dozen explosions and then a half dozen more.

'We couldn't miss,' said a track missile gunner. 'I don't think those Lebanese tankers had any idea what they were doing.'

The Lebanese were dying, scores of them, by the second. But they kept coming at our position, until the F-15s came in and attacked with laser-guided bombs. Each hit left a crater where a tank or vehicle had been. It was at that point, this reporter counted 29 separate smoke plumes, that the Lebanese finally withdrew. The Israelis kept firing.

'You cannot join the battle and then decide you don't want to fight. You can't go home. Surrender or die,' said one tank commander.

One bitter tanker summed it up thusly, 'They started it, we finished it.'

These men had seen a lot of hard fighting in the Beqaa and they resented the Lebanese late entry into the war. All would much rather have been battling Hezbollah. Other men resented the Lebanese stupidity.

'They advanced in one long line. They did not know what they were doing,' said the company commander to this reporter after the battle.

The Israelis fired on the retreating Lebanese all the way to the Beirut Damascus Highway, where the IAF took over and pounded them from the air.

'You won another battle,' this reporter said to the battalion commander.

'We did not win. We lost.'

I asked the GOC to explain.

'The only way to have won that battle was not to have fought it,' he said. 'What did we win? They were not Hezbollah. We defeated an amateur army that was not our enemy. What did we win?'

WASHINGTON DC

'Ambassador Benard?' asked the president, 'What is the precise wording of the UN resolution?'

Having flown to New York that morning and then back down to Washington that night, the ambassador looked exhausted. She yawned, 'Excuse me, Mr. President.'

'Not at all.'

'The resolution condemns the Israeli attack on Iran.'
'OK.'
'And calls for an Israeli withdrawal from Lebanon.'
'OK.'
'But it also condemns Hezbollah.'
'Good.'
'It also calls for the strengthening of the international peacekeeping force in Lebanon.'
'Fine.'
'And a task force to investigate war crimes, by both sides.'
'I can live with that.' Stettler looked at Franks, who nodded.
'The vote is tomorrow, sir.'
'Vote for it. This war stops now.'

PART III
THE PLAINES OF
DAMASCUS

CHAPTER I

ENTER GILGAMESH

MK: General Nagid, in the past you have stated that you were pleased when Syria entered the war. Do you stand by those statements today?

General Nagid: I do.

MK: May I ask why?

General Nagid: Syria's entry presented us with a once in a lifetime opportunity to engage an enemy of Israel.

MK: At great cost.

General Nagid: Do not lecture me about losses.

MK: Three hundred and fourteen dead, General.

General Nagid: Do you, my friend, have any idea what we did to the Syrians?

MK: General Nagid, you are dangerously close to being in contempt of this body.

General Nagid: That would be an accurate description of my attitude.

Testimony of General Natan Nagid Before the

Knesset Commission on the Conduct

of the War in Lebanon

DAMASCUS

The Syrian Interim Revolutionary Council was an unwieldy thing at best, with seats held by the nation's Sunni majority having to be doled out amongst the various sects within, and more seats being allotted to Syria's Kurdish, Druze, and even Christian minorities. Still the Sunnis controlled more than half the seats with a majority of these going to the old ruling Alawite sect of Sunni Islam. General Mohamed al-Arsuzi controlled the Sunni block.

General al-Arsuzi was tall, handsome, ambitious and experienced. Though an Alawite he was popular with other factions within the Sunni block and even the minorities, as he had enforced secular tolerance within the military. Sitting in his office, he listened to the massive protest taking place in the streets of Damascus, as imams led chants for the destruction of the Zionist Entity.

The wall in his Damascus office was decorated with pictures and mementos of his field commands, a commando company, later a battalion and then an armored division. On his desk he had signed photographs from the Presidents of Turkey and Egypt after serving as Syria's ambassador to those countries. He also had an American helmet, captured in Iraq, a gift from a one of the dozens of Syrian intelligence officers he had dispatched to train insurgents there.

For the past week al-Arsuzi watched in quiet admiration as the Israelis systematically destroyed Hezbollah. Destroyed was the right word, he realized. His operatives in Lebanon had been sending back startling reports saying that the damage was worse than Hezbollah was letting on, and even worse than the Israelis suspected. Several dozen Hezbollah fighters had already fled to Syria, where they were arrested on al-Arsuzi's orders, so as not to give the Israelis a pretext for invading Syria.

By all counts, the Lebanese Army Massacre, as it was now being called, was barely a battle at all. The Israeli's 162 Division had annihilated three Lebanese Army brigades in half a day. Al-Jazeera had shown footage of the northern Beqaa, a recently plowed field filled with burning Lebanese M-48 tanks. He doubted the Lebanese were able to get off a shot against the Israelis. Al-Arsuzi counted seventeen tanks in the news clip he saw. The scene looked all too familiar to a Syrian, like the Golan Heights after the October War. The memory burned al-Arsuzi.

Since the formation of the IRC a year before, al-Arsuzi had privately feared that his nation would become like Lebanon, an ethnic hodge-podge of people loyal to clan and not to state. There had been nothing to unify the various groups. For the past week the streets of Damascus had been filled with raucous protestors from all segments of Syrian society. At least for the moment, all Syrians seemed united in their hatred for Israel. If that hatred could be tapped, the nation could be unified, al-Arsuzi knew. The right man could unify the nation and make himself national savior at Israel's expense. After all, the Jews held something dear to Syrians.

On his desk al-Arsuzi had a map of the Golan Heights, and a report detailing the readiness of the Syrian armed forces. They were ready for a conflict with Israel. So was al-Arsuzi.

WASHINGTON D.C.

President Stettler looked at the front page of the *Washington Post* and was not pleased.

'It's almost as if the Israelis are trying to turn the world against them,' he said bitterly.

The right hand side of the paper showed a picture of a burning Lebanese flag amongst a cluster of destroyed and flaming vehicles. 'Lebanese Army Joints Fight', said the headline. *The New York Post* ran the same photo below a headline which more aptly described what had happened: 'Massacre' Below the fold *The Washington Post* showed a series of black and white photos of the Iranian embassy in Beirut. One photo showed trucks full of gunmen leaving the embassy. The next showed an explosion knocking down the main gate, another showed Israeli commandos storming the facility. 'Israelis Storm Iranian Embassy', read the headline, 'Pics show Hezbollah fighter, munitions'. On the bottom left of the paper was a picture of launching Katyusha rockets below the headline, 'Hezbollah Ramps up Rocket Attacks.' There was a small box in the right hand corner, which read 'UN to Vote on Resolution Today'.

'Did they have to attack the embassy?' Stettler asked.

'Well the Iranians did take credit for the Madrid and Berlin bombings,' replied Boddicker.

'Does that invalidate the Iranian's own immunity?'

'You would have to get legal ruling from the White House Council, sir.'

'Oh, Christ, does it matter anymore?'

'Probably not.'

'What do we know about what the Israelis have found in the Iranian embassy?'

'So far, tons of documents, and in the basement, weapons and rockets, not to mention Iranian Revolutionary Guard Corps soldiers. Several Hezbollah officers were there as well.'

'The world won't care,' said Stettler.

'No, sir. But neither do the Israelis anymore.'

'What are they doing today?'

'Well, sir, the battle for Beirut is ending with a whimper, not a bang. The Israelis landed another infantry brigade in the city overnight. That makes three. The Lebanese Army pulled out. Plenty of fighting with Hezbollah though, all of it very one sided.'

'Why is that?'

'Hard to say, but I would think Hezbollah used up most of its elite units in the south and in the Beqaa.'

'So the gunmen in Beirut were second rate.'

'Looks like it.'

'What about the Beqaa?' Stettler asked.

'Mostly secure.'

'And the south?'

'The same. There is sporadic resistance, nothing organized though. Israeli investigators are now finding huge caches of rockets in the south and in the Beqaa.'

'Have they defeated Hezbollah?'

'Not yet. There are still at least a few thousand fighters in the Lebanon Mountains.'

'What about their leadership?'

'We know the Israelis are investigating the bodies of several men they suspect are part of Hezbollah's senior political and military leadership, but if they have captured any such individuals alive, they are not saying.'

'In the meantime they've destroyed Lebanon.'

'Tremendous damage, yes, sir,' said Boddicker.

'What's left of the army is on the verge of mutiny,' added Davis.

'There is also a massive refugee problem developing in the north,' said Benard.

'I want us to do something about that,' said Stettler.

'Good thinking, sir,' said Franks. 'That will look good on the news.'

'Secretary Davis, I want an airlift. Relief supplies, that sort of thing. How soon can you begin?'

Davis thought for a moment, 'We'll have it in place this evening and will be able to go.'

'Good. Now ambassador Benard, what is the status of the current UN Resolution?'

'Still on track. The Iranians are screaming bloody murder,' said Benard. 'They're threatening many dire consequences if the UN does not take appropriate action.'

'What's appropriate action?' Franks asked, 'What dire consequences?'

'Closing the Straits of Hormuz, I suspect,' said Boddicker.

'Can they do that?' Franks asked.

'Only if we let them,' said Davis.

'What do we have in place?' Stettler asked.

'Two carrier battle groups, one outside the Gulf and one in the Indian Ocean and two Marine Expeditionary Units.'

'Marines?' asked Benard. 'Will they be necessary?'

'If they close the straits they may be,' said Davis.

'Uh, Mr. President, there is another issue developing,' said Boddicker.

'Something else?'

'Yes, satellites are picking up military activity. It looks as if the Syrians are mobilizing...'

JERUSALEM

The PM's hair was not quite as neat and coiffed as usual, with a few strands of grey breaking through the hair line. There were thick, dark bags under her eyes. General Ben Zvi thought the PM looked mentally exhausted. He couldn't blame her. She had spent the day on the Lebanese border, visiting various units and touring towns that had been damaged by Hezbollah rocket attacks. After that she made a speech to the Knesset. Several MKs had heckled the PM for the foreign relations catastrophe that was unfolding, with multiple condemnatory resolutions making their way through the UN, and some European nations even threatening economic sanctions and worse. That morning the Israeli attorney general had informed Eitan that prosecutors at The Hague were moving to indict her for war crimes.

The bit of news that Ben Zvi and Sedor brought the PM that evening seemed to visibly break her spirits.

'Are you sure?' Eitan demanded.

'Yes,' said both men in unison.

To Ben Zvi it looked as if Eitan wanted to slump down on her desk and hold her head in her hands. If he were PM, he would want to do the same. He was glad he wasn't a politician.

'What are your intelligence sources?'

'Human, within Syria,' said Sedor. 'Electronic eavesdropping.'

'Prime Minister, our observers on the Golan can see the Syrians moving. There are huge concentrations of tanks and vehicles to the east.'

'Prime Minister,' began Sedor, 'on my own orders I sent several drones over Syrian airbases. They are abuzz with activity. Aircraft are fueling and arming.'

'Could this just be sabre rattling?'

'No, Prime Minister,' Ben Zvi replied. 'This is not sabre rattling. The bluster coming out of Damascus a week ago was sabre rattling. This is war preparation.'

'How long?'

'They will be ready to attack within 24 hours.'

'Do you want to attack first?' she asked.

'While we do have plans for such a contingency,' began Ben Zvi, 'with the fighting in Lebanon we are not currently prepared to do so.'

'Why are they doing this?' Eitan asked.

Sedor spoke. 'We have an extensive dossier on al-Arsuzi. He was not well known during the previous regime. He spent much time overseas.'

'So his hands were relatively clean.'

'For a Syrian general, yes,' said Sedor. 'He is popular within the army. He rooted out political officers from the old regime and instituted a rapid retraining program. He also emphasized pride and identity.'

'How so?'

'He's made much of the nation's Assyrian and Babylonian past and talked much about Syrian victories against us in '73 and '82.'

Eitan snorted.

'Snort all you like, Prime Minister,' said Ben Zvi, 'The Syrians were the most disciplined and tenacious fighters the IDF fought in '73. I fought them in the Beqaa in 1982.'

'So we have to let them attack us?'

'I believe so.'

'Are we prepared for that?'

'Right now we have one reserve division atop the Golan Heights, three brigades in all. Twelve brigades are in Lebanon right now. Four more along our northern border.'

'Is that enough?'

'What I would like to do is send Division162 to the Golan. I want to make the move very public.'

'Why?'

'Doing so might dissuade the Syrians.'

'Alright,' said Eitan. 'Do it.'

General Ben Zvi stood. 'With your permission Prime Minister, I must consult with General Nagid.'

'Nagid,' the prime minister smiled wearily.

TEL NOF

'Are you serious?'

'Yes, General Peled, this is serious,' replied the air force chief.

'Why Maccabee Force?'

'The rest of the air force has been fighting for days. Your men and aircraft are rested.'

'Yes, after a week's hard work,' protested Peled.

'What is there for me to say, General?' replied the chief, 'The Syrians are on their way.'

'What are my orders?'

'The prime minister and cabinet gave one order. Clear skies over Israel.'

'Lovely time for a slogan,' remarked Peled. 'May I enter Syrian airspace?'

'Clear skies over Israel. Do what you have to do.'

'Understood.'

'Good luck, General.'

'Thank you, Chief.'

Peled spent the next hour issuing orders for Maccabee Force to ready. He knew that sixty-eight F-16s at Ramat David and Tel Nof could be put in the air within an hour. He sat at his desk and on a blank piece of paper wrote down the strength of the Syrian air force, number of squadrons, types of jets, known readiness. He knew the Syrian Air Force order of battle by heart. He thought for several minutes about how he would commit that force to battle, and then thought about how a Syrian general would commit that force.

'They will muck it up,' he concluded.

CHAPTER II

ABOVE AND BEYOND THE GOLAN

MK: What was your intention, General Nagid?

General Nagid: What was my intention, you ask?

MK: Yes, General.

General Nagid: My intention was to destroy the Syrian army at the first opportunity.

MK: And when they gave that opportunity you acted.

General Nagid: Absolutely. Without hesitation.

Testimony of General Natan Nagid before the

Knesset Committee on the Conduct

of the war in Lebanon

I say this as a military man, but also as an air war historian, what Maccabee Force accomplished over the Golan Heights is one of the greatest victories in the history of air warfare.

General Benny Peled, *Three Missions*

THE GOLAN HEIGHTS

Gonzo and Gilden clung to the back of a Merkeva tank as Division 162 climbed the west slope of the Golan Heights. He reviewed the quick notes he had taken from the men of the tank platoon they'd been embedded with. They were tired, but most seemed almost giddy at the thought of fighting a real tank battle against a real army.

'Does that make any sense?' Gonzo asked.

'Well, think about it,' said Gilden. 'You, me, all these guys were raised on stories of the great battles in the Sinai and the Golan.'

'So?'

'So?' Gilden repeated, 'These men are tankers. There hasn't been a major armored battle in more than 40 years. That's a great angle for a story you know.'

'You think so?'

'Think of the headline - modern tankers eager to prove mettle.'

Gonzo returned to his notes.

Gilden tugged Gonzo's arm. 'Hey look at that.'

He pointed skyward to a half dozen missile contrails streaking toward Israel.

'And look at that!' Gilden remarked as an Israeli Arrow Missile blew a Syrian Scud out of the sky.

'Yes, but three more are going through,' said Gonzo.

There was another explosion in the sky, a burst of light and a cloud of smoke and debris above the Golan. A second later there was another such explosion.

'There's a third!' shouted Gilden.

'That fourth missile looks like it's headed for Haifa,' said Gonzo.

Gonzo tracked the missile's progress until Gilden nudged him again and pointed east, 'Look at that!' he shouted.

Flying at a few thousand feet was a line of contrails, eight in all, and behind that another line of ten.

'What are those?' Gonzo asked. 'Katysushas?'

'Looks like it.'

'I guess we're at war with Syria now.'

'When you're already at war with Iran and Lebanon, what's one more country?' Gilden asked.

Under an increasingly intense barrage of Katyusha and Scud missiles, the division pushed east across the Golan. They drove past Several farms and kibbutzim, all seemed to be abandoned. More than halfway across the heights, the brigade halted. They pulled over to the side of the road. Minutes later units of the 900th Brigade began passing them.

'Hey, how come we're stopped?' Gonzo asked the tank commander, who sat in his cupola smoking cigarettes as tanks and APCs drove past.

The tank commander shrugged. 'Not my decision.'

'Are we to be held in reserve?'

The tank commander shrugged.

They heard the distant sound of artillery rounds in the air followed by explosions. The barrage continued. Gonzo could see wisps of smoke rising to the east.'

'What's that?'

'The Syrians.'

NORTHERN ISRAEL

'General Nagid,' said the Golan sector commander, 'the Syrians are advancing across a broad, three division front.'

'Three divisions?' Nagid asked.

'Yes.'

'Good.'

'My front line commanders report that the Syrians are sending infantry first, each of my bunkers is being attacked by rocket and missile teams. Artillery is starting to come into play.'

'What about their tanks and armored vehicles?'

'Coming up behind the infantry. My men need reinforcements if they are to hold the Purple Line.'

'No, no!' Nagid shouted into the phone. 'Tell the battalions on the Golan to pull back.'

'Pull back?' responded the very confused Golan sector commander.

'They can't stop the Syrians, and I do not want them to.'

'Then what are my men's orders?' asked the commander.

'Retreat in good order,' replied Nagid. 'Division 162 is behind you. This is why I kept them in the Beqaa. Now get out of their way.'

'Yes, sir.'

Nagid handed the phone back to his aide.

'Get this report to Division 162.'

'General, there is also the matter of Hezbollah forces trapped between our own units and the Lebanon Mountains.'

'What of it?'

'Various news agencies report that the UN is putting out feelers about a ceasefire and evacuation.'

'Like the Church of the Nativity Siege of 2002?'

'Something like that. Yes, sir. There's talk of exile to Cyprus.'

Nagid shook his head. 'Not this time.'

NORTH BEIRUT

As he looked at the map, for the first time the Hornet felt actual dismay. The Jews more or less controlled Beirut. Even worse, resistance in the south had been utterly crushed, even his mortar squads were gone, destroyed down to the last man by Israeli hunter/killer teams. Rocket fire had fallen to an almost negligible pace, and those that were fired were smaller caliber Katysuahs. Every time Hezbollah tried to deploy a long range rocket launcher the truck carrying it was pounced upon by Israeli aircraft. The south and center of Israel were now completely immune to rocket attacks. He had more than a thousand men at the foot of the Lebanon Mountains. They were trapped and there was little the Hornet could do to help, much less save them.

The Jews were less than a mile away from his villa, the Hornet knew, but he dared not move. The sky was filled with aircraft, jets, helicopters, and if one looked closely, drones. They were watching everything. He didn't even take his morning stroll on the beach. The fishing village to the north had been shelled by a pair of Zionist ships, and the boats there sunk. Nor did he swim his laps. He didn't want to anyway. Since the power went out the pool had developed a thin layer of algae, it was filled with leaves and other debris as well.

'Where's the pool boy?' the Hornet asked the old lady. 'Where is Yasser?'

LEBANON

From his position two miles west of the Lebanon Mountains, Beta watched as yet another pair of Israeli jets pounded the western slope. Through his binoculars he saw a pair of huge explosions as laser-guided bombs impacted on an entrance to what was believed to be a bunker complex deep underground. There was no return fire from Hezbollah.

'How long are we going to wait here, Sergeant?' asked one of his men.

'We wait until the commander tells us to advance.'

'Any idea when that will be?'

Beta glared at the eager paratrooper but said nothing.

Beta turned back to the conflagration of smoke and fire. He watched until 1700 hours, when word came down to ready the men. At 1730 the paratroopers came out of their dugouts and advanced. Beta looked behind him and saw the sun approaching the horizon. It would be in the eyes of Hezbollah fighters.

They walked across an open field. Beta looked left and right and could see hundreds of paratroopers arrayed in a ragged line on either side. Beyond these were dust clouds as tanks moved forward as well. Ahead of them were dozens of artillery smoke plumes. Artillery shells and rockets roared above and slammed into the base of the Lebanon Mountains.

For twenty minutes nothing happened. They walked through a field, then past a smashed farm house. Then, beyond the house, they approached an olive grove. When they got to within a hundred yards of the grove Hezbollah fighters within unleashed a torrent of small arms and RPG fire. Beta and his men hit the deck and returned fire. The tanks behind them opened up as well, lacing the grove with frag shells which tore up trees and men alike. An anti-tank missile streaked out from the grove but flew right over one of the tanks. Beta and his men spotted the launch position and brought it under fire. An Israeli mortar barrage landed on the far side of the grove, catching several Hezbollah fighters as they tried to pull back. From there Beta's company advanced to the edge of the olive grove and then through it. Beta walked past a young Hezbollah fighter, his right leg and arm blown off from a shell burst. He had quickly bled to death. He almost tripped on another that had been decapitated.

At the far edge of the grove they took more small arms fire, this time from a line of Hezbollah fighters in a drainage ditch. The paratroopers once again took cover and returned fire as the tanks slowly advanced. When these emerged the Hezbollah fighters fired a few RPGs, but these missed wildly. The tanks tore up the ditch with a barrage of frag rounds, and when the gunners were finished there was nothing left of the Hezbollah fighters. The paratroopers advanced once more.

Beta didn't let his men stop at the drainage ditch, and they kept going into the field beyond. Once more they took fire from Hezbollah fighters, this time from a row of chicken coops on the far side the field. The tanks blasted these to bits. Beyond that was a wheat field. As Beta and his men approached, with tanks coming up behind them, several men emerged from the field. They walked slowly, their hands in the air. A few of them waved white flags.

'Stop!' Beta shouted in Arabic.

The men stopped.

'Take your shirts off!'

The fighters, they all looked young to Beta, looked at each other. After a few seconds hesitation, Beta shouted again, 'Take your shirts off or we shoot you where you stand!'

The fighters stripped down to their waists.

'Now drop your pants!'

This time the fighters did as they were told, dropping their pants around their ankles.

'Well, no suicide bombers,' said one of the paratroopers.

'They could have something shoved up their asses,' said Beta.

'I think you are being paranoid, Sergeant. I do not believe these boys have that kind of dedication.'

Beta nodded. 'Alright! Come forward!'

There were small arms fire to the right, as a platoon there engaged a Hezbollah position.

The Hezbollah fighters, pants around their ankles, awkwardly shuffled forward. When they got to within ten yards Beta ordered them to the ground. His paratroopers fanned out and bound the fighter's hands behind their back and sat them up. There were seven in all. They looked filthy and tired.

'Water?' one asked.

Beta took his canteen off his belt and held it to the man's lips. He drank gratefully.

'These guys stink,' said one of the paratroopers.

Beta's earpiece cracked, 'Keep moving, Beta,' said the platoon commander, 'Leave the prisoners for the follow on troops.'

'Yes, lieutenant.' Beta turned to his squad and shouted, 'Alright, men, we keep moving!' Beta shouted.

The artillery barrages on the Lebanon Mountains intensified.

WASHINGTON, DC

Boddicker sat in the Oval Office and watched the television with the president, Franks, Davis and Benard. He had to restrain himself from shouting 'Yes!' and pumping his fist in the air. Instead he said, 'The Israelis are finishing the job. I think----'

Franks cut him off, 'Quiet!'

The BBC anchor spoke.

'It now appears, despite international efforts to mediate a settlement with the hundreds, if not thousands of Hezbollah fighters trapped against the Lebanon Mountains, the Israelis are continuing the attack.'

'Yes, that is right, Martin,' said a reporter on the other side of split screen. Behind him were the Lebanon Mountains, now partially obscured by smoke. A pair of Apache helicopters made their way across the distant sky. There were yellow flashes on the ground below them.

'What have the Israelis done?' asked the anchor.

'As the sun went down, their forces began advancing east. Tanks, APCs and infantry closed in on the trapped Hezbollah fighters.'

"Is Hezbollah fighting back?'

'Absolutely. The term heavy fighting is often misused but here it is highly appropriate. The Israeli advance has encountered fierce resistance.'

The anchor struck a tone of concern, 'Are there heavy casualties?'

'No way to say for certain, but there is every reason to believe that both sides are suffering.'

'Have the Israelis taken into account international moves to bring about a ceasefire?'

'Honestly, I do not think they care anymore. The mood among Israeli officers I spoke…'

The president finally spoke. 'I'm not sure I would allow Hezbollah out of that trap.'

'Nor I, Mr. President,' said Boddicker.

'Wonderful,' said Benard.

'Why do you say that?' asked Boddicker.

'This is leaving a diplomatic mess. I'm going to have to try to fix this.'

'What are the Europeans going to say?' asked Stettler.

'They're already screaming about war crimes. I...'

Boddicker interrupted. 'How much worse can it get?'

Before Benard could respond, Stettler said, 'He has a point.'

KING KHALID MILITARY CITY

Prince Abdullah paused his speech as the camera panned to the wreckage lying on the hanger floor. The television monitor in front of him showed the camera locked on the Star of David on the wing of the jet wreckage. Once a few seconds had elapsed, he resumed his speech.

'Brothers, I come to tell you that we have been betrayed. The new monarchy has allowed the Jews to fly over sacred Muslim land to attack our fellow Muslims. I call on all Muslims to take to the streets and resist the satanic alliance between the new monarchy and the Jews....'

GOLAN HEIGHTS

As the Syrian attack on the Golan began, Gonzo and Gilden sat in the back of the turret, listening and taking notes as the tank commander and his crew fought their tank.

Syrian artillery came first, but the barrages fell far short of the Israeli line. A few minutes after the artillery ceased the Israelis spotted Syrian infantry and APCs advancing. Bullets bounced off the hull of the Merkeva tank. The tank's driver fired his .30 caliber machine gun in response. The tank commander left his MG alone and instead spotted for the gunner.

'Gunner, target, APC, five-five-zero yards.'

There was a distant wooshing sound and then another followed by an explosion.

'What was that?' Gonzo asked.

'Shut up,' replied the tank commander. 'Anti-tank missiles.'

'Target identified,' said the gunner.

'Fire.'

'On the way!' replied the gunner.

The gunner pressed the trigger sending an explosive shell hurtling out the barrel. A second later the gunner reported, 'Target destroyed!'

The tank commander looked through his site, 'Confirmed.'

There was another whooshing sound.

'RPG,' said the commander.

Gonzo listened to the chatter of the platoon radio net as more tanks reported targets engaged and destroyed.

The radio squawked. 'Get those APCs forward,' said the platoon commander. 'We cannot deal with these missile gunners.'

'Company says tracks are moving up.'

'I see one,' said the tank commander.

'Where?' asked the driver.

'About thirty meters. Wait, there he goes, hold on.'

The tank commander remote fired his .50 caliber. 'Follow my tracers,' he said.

'I see them,' responded the driver.

The two men fired their machine guns.

'I think we got him,' said the TC.

Over the radio someone said, 'APCs in line now, firing.'

Gonzo could hear the rip of heavy machine guns.

'You want to have a look?' the tank commander asked Gonzo.

'Sure.'

'Quickly.'

Gonzo stepped forward and put his eyes to the commander's site. He saw several burning APCs. There were also muzzle flashes. Syrian infantry no doubt. He actually saw a man fall to the ground as a burst from one of the Israeli APCs caught him. Behind the burnt-out Syrian APCs, he could see movement.

'Hey I see something back there.'

The tank commander grabbed Gonzo by the shoulder and pushed him away. 'Back,' he said.

Gonzo heard the roar of jet engines overhead.

'Looks like the air force is here,' said the tank commander.

'Ours or theirs?'

'Both.'

RAMAT DAVID

Peled and his ground staff gathered in the command bunker at Ramat David. Once more the air control officers stood before a quartet of ground controllers, all under the direction of Colonel Avi. Computer screens and flat screen monitors showed the unfolding air battle, the largest Israel had fought in nearly four decades.

The Syrians began the air battle by scrambling their squadrons of antiquated Mig-21 fighters. Within half an hour three dozen Migs were in the air and forming up over their airbases. As they banked toward the Golan and Israel, Peled released four F-16 sections, sixteen jets in all, to engage. A massive dog fight erupted in the sky of the Golan Heights.

As the first waves engaged, the Syrians scrambled their squadrons of more advanced fighter aircraft, amounting to 23 Mig-25s, 21 Mig-23s and a dozen Mig-29s.

'So, they're using the Mig-21s as cannon fodder for the advanced aircraft,' Peled said.

Peled had planned for such a contingency, and kept Maccabee Force's two sections of F-15 Eagles in reserve. Already in the air, he pushed these to the edge of the Golan, where they launched standoff long-range missile attacks on the still forming Syrian Migs. The first volley of missiles downed four Syrian aircraft, the next volley accounted for another three. After that the remaining Mig pilots broke east, away from the Israeli jets.

Over Maccabbee Force's radio net, the two F-15 sections commanders asked for permission to pursue. Peled grabbed a microphone from the console and said, 'Negative, maintain position.'

He looked at the flat screen showing the radar readout of the battle above the Golan. One blue icon was leaving the battle area and returning to Ramat David.

'What is wrong with that aircraft?' Peled asked.

'Minor damage to the fuselage, General,' said Colonel Avi.

'What are their losses?'

'There is a kill tally in the bottom left corner of the screen, General.'

'Ah.'

The tally, blue for Israel and red for Syria showed 11-0 in Israel's favor. As Peled looked on, the tally moved up to twelve, and then a moment later thirteen and fourteen.

'The Syrians are just throwing their jets into the battle, piecemeal,' Avi said.

They continued doing so. New red icons appeared over two Syrian airfields east of Damascus.

'What kind of aircraft are those?' Peled asked.

'Looks like more Mig-21s. Three and four aircraft so far.'

'Order the F-15 sections to engage from standoff points.'

'Yes, sir.'

Each F-15 section fired another volley of missiles. Peled watched the tiny blue icons until they merged with the red icons above the airstrip. Three more hits.

'Hit them again,' ordered Peled.

'That will be the F-15s last volley.'

'Understood.'

The air control officer passed the order down to the F-15 sections. Seconds later the last volley of eight medium range missiles was fired and in the air. Four more Syrian Migs were downed. The kill tally showed 16-0 in Israel's favor.

'What orders for the F-15 sections?' asked Avi.

'Tell them to land and rearm.'

'Yes, sir.'

'General, Syrian Migs are still scrambling.'

'Yes, I know.'

'Shall we send some F-16s into Syrian airspace to engage?'

The kill tally read 17-0.

'No.'

'But we could catch them as they try to scramble.'

18-0.

'No. We risk losing aircraft to Syrian SAM batteries. I do not want to manage a search and rescue effort while most of the army is engaged in Lebanon and on the Golan.'

'I understand.'

'Colonel, feed F-16 sections into the Golan battle as the need arises.'

'Yes, General.'

There was little for Peled to do other than watch as the battle raged over the Golan Heights. The Syrians kept fighting despite losses. After an hour those losses amounted to 30 aircraft. When the Israeli F-15s returned to Tel Nof, the squadrons of Syrian Mig-25s and Mig-29s raced from their positions over eastern Syria to the Golan and joined the battle there. Colonel Avi vectored a pair of F-16 sections against them. Another dogfight ensued, this one just east of the Golan. After ten minutes the Israelis had downed six Migs without suffering losses. The Mig-25s and Mig-29s withdrew again. Once more Peled had to rein in the section commanders. Instead of pursuing the Migs, Peled ordered the F-16s sections rerouted into the Golan aerial battle. At that point, the Syrian pilots there withdrew. As the more advanced Migs flew east, another wave of Mig-21s passed them and joined the Golan battle.

The tally read 34-0 in favor of Israel.

'Where are those Migs going?' Peled asked.

'Well, several are landing...'

'But that trio heading north? Are they making for Turkey?'

'Hmmm ...' said Avi as he looked at the screen. 'It looks so.'

Two more Migs went down over the Golan.

'General, new contacts over central Syria...' said a radar tech, 'Three icons appeared on the radar readout over central Syria. 'Each of three Mig-21s.'

'F-15s back on station,' reported Colonel Avi.

'Order them to engage the targets. Long range standoff attack,' ordered Peled.

The first volley downed three Migs over central Syria. That was enough for the other pilots, who banked to starboard and sped north.

'They're not stopping,' said Avi.

'Look at this!' shouted one of the radar techs.

'What is it?' asked Peled.

'A flight of Mig-21s scrambled and broke north.'

'How many,' asked Peled.

'Six, all breaking north.'

'What about the Golan battle?' asked Peled.

'I see three Migs now breaking off....now a fourth...now a fifth.'

'What does it mean?' asked Avi.

'They're afraid to fight us,' Peled said. 'How many have we shot down?'

Colonel Avi looked at the tally for the Golan and added to the other number of kills. 'Sixty one.'

'Make that sixty three, sir,' said the radar tech. 'Two more just went down above the Golan.

They watched as the remaining Migs above the Golan disengaged in twos and threes. After several minutes the sky above was uncontested. Several pairs of F-16s were now running east in pursuit.

'Order those F-16s back,' said Peled.

'Yes, sir.'

'They don't want to fight. We will not give them a reason to change their mind.'

DAMASCUS

General al-Arsuzi slammed his fist on the desk in rage. 'Deserters!' he shouted. 'They are actually deserting the battlefield!'

'I am sorry, General,' said the air force commander, one of al-Arsuzi's handpicked men.

'I don't care if you are sorry.'

'Yes, General.'

'How many aircraft have we lost to Turkey?'

'So far, eleven that we know of.'

The general composed himself and said. 'Round up three of the deserting pilots that have returned to our airfields and execute them.'

'Sir?'

'I said execute them.'

'Sir.'

'I want this done by tonight.'

'Yes, sir.'

He turned to his ground force commander, another handpicked man, who until then had stood by impassively. 'What news of the Golan battle?'

WASHINGTON DC

'So let me see if I have this correct,' Stettler began 'Syria and Israel are fighting on the Golan.'

'Yes,' replied Boddicker.

'Are these skirmishes?'

'No, it's a full-on armored battle.'

'Four divisions, one Israeli, three Syrian,' said Davis. 'More than a thousand tanks in total.'

'Jesus,' said Stettler.

'He's not on the Golan right now, sir,' Boddicker remarked dryly. Stettler gave Boddicker an icy stare.

'On top of that, there is now some kind of revolution in Saudi Arabia.'

'Yes, sir.'

Stettler threw his hands in the air. 'What the hell is this about?'

'Prince Abdullah has accused the new king of allowing Israel to use Saudi airspace to attack Iran.'

'Is it true?'

'Well, they do have a wrecked fuselage,' said Boddicker.

'And the confession of the commander of their air defense network.'

The news channels were running the commander's taped confession over and over again. He was handcuffed and blindfolded in a dark room, and according to the translator saying, 'Yes, I allowed the Zionists into our Muslim land.'

'Do you believe his confession?' Benard asked.

Boddicker shook his head.

'They're macabre bastards, aren't they?' Benard said.

'Yes, Ma'am,' said Boddicker.

Stettler waved his hand. 'Alright, quiet. Boddicker, what is happening right now over there?'

'Massive protests beginning in major cities like Riyadh, Mecca and Jiddah. So far the army is in barracks.'

'Is that good or bad?' Stettler asked.

'I'd say good,' said Boddicker. 'It says Abdullah and the army are working together.'

'To oust the king?'

'Yes, sir.'

'Well, ever since the new king took the throne he's been saying bizarre things about world conspiracies, Zionists, he's…'

'Bonkers, yes, sir,' said Boddicker.

'What about the prince?'

'Not bonkers,' said Boddicker.

Stettler laughed a little. 'Thanks.'

'Western educated, time in DC and London. Served in their armed forces. A moderate by Saudi standards.'

'Yes, but what does he want?'

'To be king.'

'OK. What will he do after that?'

'Well, there doesn't seem to be much of a point in having a revolution just to maintain the status-quo.'

THE GOLAN HEIGHTS

Gonzo wiped soot from his face and coughed up dust, only to look up and get choked by smoke from a burning Merkeva. He ducked until the smoke subsided and then peered through the haze. The Merkeva tank on their right had taken two hits. One shell blasted the left track so that it slumped down and forward toward Gonzo. One of the crewmen from the Merkava dragged a body behind the tank. The second shell that hit the Merkeva glanced left off its armor and blew the tank commander, who had been standing in the cuploa reloading his .50 caliber, right off the tank and decapitated Gilden, who had been standing next to him.

'Do you see his head?' asked the gunner.

A line of artillery shells exploded to the rear.

'No,' Gonzo said.

'Alright, well, help me with the rest of him.'

Two crewmen pushed Gilden's body up out of the turret. Gonzo took hold of the collar, which was covered in blood and goo. 'Pull!' shouted the gunner.

The trio pushed and pulled until Gilden's body was out of the turret. From there they manhandled the body onto the engine deck.

'Help me get him down to the ground.'

Gonzo took the legs. When they got Gilden down to the ground, he asked. 'You just going to leave him here?'

'He's dead, isn't he?'

Gonzo shrugged.

'Come on.'

Gonzo and the loader climbed back into the tank.

'Well, we're a little less crowded,' the gunner dryly remarked. He was about to say something else, but before he could, orders came across the platoon radio net.

'Copy that, Lieutenant,' he said to the platoon commander.

'What's happening? Gonzo asked.

'We are advancing!' the gunner said with mock enthusiasm.

'Advancing?' Gonzo asked.

'Yes. Have you ever been to Syria?'

'Ummm…no.'

'Well, here's your chance!'

After a few minutes on the move Gonzo said, 'Hey I thought you said we were going to Syria.'

'We are.'

'Well, that's mount Hermon up there. We're heading north, not east.'

JERUSALEM

'Division 162 is advancing?' asked an incredulous Eitan. 'Is this on the orders of General Nagid?'

'Yes, Prime Minister,' replied General Ben Zvi.

'Not your orders?'

'No, Prime Minister.'

'And certainly not mine.'

'No.'

'Can we stop him?

'General Nagid issued the order. An hour later he informed me. Once I learned of that order I came here to inform you.'

'Are you saying there is not time left to turn back Division 162?'

'I do not think so.'

'By now elements have come down from the Golan and are approaching the Damascus Plain, where an Israeli armoured division will, single handedly, engage the bulk of the Syrian army.'

'Can they win?'

'The division turned back an attack by elements of three Syrian divisions this morning.'

'You have not answered the question.'

'No, Prime Minister, I haven't answered because I do not know the answer.'

'Events are out of our hands, aren't they?'

'Prime Minister, events have been out of our control for some time.'

Eitan waved her hands in frustration. 'Send him all the help he needs.'

DAMASCUS

Al-Arsuzi was pleased with the report being delivered.

'After halting our advance in the morning, the Jews are retreating back several kilometers.'

'What is the status of our forces?' al-Arsuzi asked.

'Heavy casualties in all three divisions, at least half of our tanks lost. They are now suffering from intermittent air attacks.'

'Where are our two reserve divisions?'

'Assembled south and west of Damascus, sir.'

'Order them to the Golan.'

'Yes, sir.'

'If we can establish ourselves as a fact on the ground there, we've won.'

THE DAMASCUS PLAIN

'Traverse left!" ordered the platoon commander.

The entire platoon of Merkeva tanks traversed left, bringing it face to face with a Syrian rocket battery.

Gonzo watched as the gunner grabbed hold of the turret mounted .50-caliber machine gun, trained it on the Syrian truck to his front and opened fire. 50 caliber rounds slammed into the truck, popping tires, and blowing the engine hood open. Eventually a round hit the gas tank and the truck exploded. Other tanks in the platoon trained their main guns on the Syrian rocket launchers. AP rounds destroyed the launchers and the missiles mounted on them, sending huge fireballs into the sky above. Within seconds the battery of four rocket launchers was reduced to flaming steel.

As the platoon slowly made its way through the wreckage, Gonzo looked to his right, back toward the Golan. There were explosions in that direction as Israeli forces engaged the Syrian rear echelon elements. To the east, toward Damascus, he could make out the rest of Division 162, two brigades, as they pushed toward the city. The Beirut/ Damascus Highway was just ahead of them.

They emerged on the other side of the now wrecked missile battery to see a vast open plain, dotted by only a few small ridges and the Beirut/ Damascus Highway.

'Holy crap!' said the gunner.

Gonzo looked forward. About a kilometer away was the highway. From east to west it was packed with tanks, trucks, and armored vehicles - crawling along the road bumper to bumper to the Golan.

'Target, dead ahead!' shouted the gunner.

Without waiting for the order, the gunner fired. A few seconds later a Syrian APC exploded in a ball of flame. The other tanks in the platoon fired, destroying three more Syrian vehicles in quick succession. The gunner looked at Gonzo. 'Get down there and load!' He pushed Gonzo down into the turret.

'AP!' the gunner shouted at Gonzo.

'Huh?'

'A-P!' he shouted again. The loader pointed to one shell storage locker. 'This holds AP rounds!' He pointed to the next locker. 'This holds HE. This one over here holds Frag. Got it!'

'I don't know anything about loading it.'

'Like this!' In frustration the gunner pressed a lever on the turret floor which opened the AP storage locker, took a shell out, and slammed it into the breach of the main gun. 'It is not rocket science, see!'

'I see."

The gunner got back in his seat, lined up a Syrian tank, and fired.

The gun breach flew back and spit out a spent shell.

'AP!' the gunner shouted.

Gonzo hit the floor peddle, grabbed an AP shell and slammed it into the breach.

'There you go.'

Gonzo heard the company commander on the radio, 'What is going on down there?!'

The platoon commander responded. 'We just found half the Syrian army in front of us!'

'Do not exaggerate.'

'Come see for yourself.'

'I am coming down to your position now.'

'Good, Captain, bring the whole company, and then the battalion. And whoever else you can find.'

Minutes later, when the company commander had joined the platoon's skirmish line, he reported back to battalion. 'Yes, that is right, hundreds, thousands of vehicles here. Must be a division or more.'

'Do you want to retreat?' the battalion commander asked.

'Hell no, we're tankers.'

'You're too weak to defend against them.'

'Then we'll attack!'

RAMAT DAVID

'General, a Syrian column is strung out along the Syrian side of the Beirut/Damascus Highway. Reports say bumper to bumper, miles long.'

'What do we have on the tarmac?'

'Six F-16s.'

'Get them armed and ready.'

'Another two dozen are returning now.'

'Very well. Refuel and arm them with bombs as they come in. Send them back out as they're ready.'

'Yes, General Peled.'

'Send everything, absolutely everything.'

WASHINGTON DC

Stettler lay down on the couch and closed his eyes.

'At least the resolution passed the Security Council,' he said.

Having cleared the Security Council, the General Assembly was sure to adopt Resolution 2016 which called for a ceasefire, UN peace-keepers and a board of inquiry to investigate war crimes. Stettler was trying not to think about the other resolutions coming to the floor when he drifted off. A few minutes later the phone rang. He rolled over onto his stomach and wondered why the First Lady wasn't answering the phone. As the ring persisted, Stettler finally pulled himself up and picked up the phone on the table next to the couch. It was Franks.

'God damn it, Franks, can I get five fucking minutes to myself?'

'I'm sorry to bother you, Mr. President. But you need to see this.'

'See what?'

'Put it on MTV.'

'Is this a joke?'

'Afraid not, sir.'

Stettler turned on the TV, but didn't know what channel MTV was on. '334 on your system, sir,' Franks said.

He turned to MTV. There was Kelly conducting an interview with two good-looking, photogenic people, a young man and young woman in military uniforms. A box in the corner proclaimed LIVE EXCLUSIVE.

'Oh dear Lord,' Stettler said.

'Yes, sir.'

Stettler turned his attention to the TV, where, apparently, his daughter was interviewing two Israeli soldiers.

'Let me just tell you,' she said, 'I think it's totally OK what you guys are doing…'

NORTHERN ISRAEL

It was with great pleasure that Nagid read Gonzo's story which was splashed across the front page of *Haaretz*. He especially smiled at the location.

Syria- It has already been named the Highway of Tears.

Yesterday, Israeli forces advancing deep into Syria, encountered what is estimated to be two entire Syrian mechanized divisions making their way toward the Golan. Lead elements of the Israeli advance brought the massive Syrian column under fire, first a platoon then a company followed by an entire battalion of Merkeva tanks. Soon, the whole brigade was committed to the fight.

The Syrians did not realize we were on their right flank until it was too late. What happened next was a massacre. Syrian vehicles exploded in ones and twos, creating a great junk yard of military equipment which bottlenecked the Beirut/Damascus Highway well short of the Golan. At least one Syrian division was now trapped behind the wreckage.

While the brigade fanned out, with two battalions branching west to deal with Syrian forces on that side of the highway, Israeli jets arrived over the battlefield. The jets came in dribs and drabs. A Falcon would drop a pair of gravity bombs along the highway and dart back west, then another would make a run at the highway. Soon the trickle of jets became a stream as more and more Israeli F-16s joined the fray. Then Israeli helicopters arrived on the scene, tank-busting Apaches armed with armor-piercing cannons and anti-tank missiles. They lashed the ground with great streams of fire. As the sun fell toward the horizon the Beirut/Damascus Highway became a great flaming trail of death snaking through the Syrian plain.

With the highway aflame, and Syrian troops on the Golan trapped between two Israeli forces, the remaining pair of Israeli brigades advanced to the heights overlooking Damascus. A line of Merkeva tanks, proudly flying the Star of David from their antennas, trained their guns on Syrian forces below and blasted all before them. Using night vision equipment their barrage continued unimpeded throughout the night claiming surface to air missile batteries, supply depots, and the military airbase below the heights.

Israeli jets also struck military and government targets in Damascus proper….

Nagid put the paper down. Behind him, the TV was tuned to al-Jazera. A correspondent for the network talked to a reporter on the ground in Damascus, who stood before a flaming building, said to be the Syrian Ministry of Information. In the corner was a box showing a live feed of the aforementioned military airstrip. Every building was in flames.

Nagid Smiled. *I've destroyed five Syrian divisions in a day.*

He ruminated on his standing in Israeli military history until interrupted by one of his aides.

'We have the report on Operation Eleventh Plague for you, sir.'

Nagid took the report.

'It just needs your signature, and then we'll send it to the prime minister.'

'No,' replied, Nagid. 'I will deliver it myself.'

Nagid began reading. He smiled once more.

WASHINGTON DC

'No no,' said Svetlana Dysenko, 'the president had no knowledge of his daughter's plans to interview the two Israel spokespersons.'

'But how could he not know?' asked Red Dye Job.

'The president has been quite busy lately, as I'm sure you know. He does not have his daughter's television schedule.'

'Don't you think he should be concerned about his daughter's actions?' Red Dye Job demanded.

'I think the American people are much more concerned about events in the Middle East than they are about MTV programming, don't you?'

Aggressive Blonde interjected, 'What of the protests now coming from the Middle East. Since the broadcast, the Turks and the

Palestinian Authority are accusing the president of working with the Israelis...'

RIYADH

'What news?'

'The king is in the palace. He is surrounded.'

'Not by soldiers.'

Rafah smiled. 'No, by an angry mob. At least 50,000 are there.'

'Very good.'

'Mob leaders are threatening to stay for months if need be. Tents are being pitched and food passed out. I am quietly having these delivered by army trucks.'

'Can a mob really have leaders, Cousin?'

General Rafah smiled. 'This one does.'

'Good.'

'What next?'

'We wait a few days. Then it will be time for a martyr.'

JERUSALEM

General Nagid walked into the cabinet room and saluted. Waiting for him were Eitan, Alon, and General Ben Zvi.

'Please sit, General,' said Eitan.

Nagid took a seat at the opposite end of the table. 'Shall I begin?' The other three nodded.

'The battle of central Lebanon has been a tremendous success. In the last thirty six hours we have killed a further 317 Hezbollah fighters.

'You are sure of this?' asked Eitan.

'We are updating the body count website now. We have names, ranks, and in more than half the cases, addresses, Prime Minister.'

'Go on,' said Eitan.

'We captured or destroyed seventy six launchers and more than four hundred rockets of various calibers.'

Ben Zvi spoke. 'The rocket fire has slackened, Prime Minister.'

'There were twenty-two rocket impacts within Israel as of this morning, General,' she scolded. 'Proceed, General Nagid.'

'We have four hundred-ninety four prisoners. These are being interrogated right now.' He turned to Sedor. 'I expect to have a preliminary report to you this afternoon. There should be much actionable intelligence.'

'I hope so,' said Sedor.

'We already have a trio of heliborne teams moving on what we have learned.'

'Good,' said Eitan. 'What of Beirut?'

'Sporadic fighting within.'

'Casualties?'

'As of this morning, we have suffered fifty-one dead and seventy-two wounded.'

'That's just in Beirut,' said Alon.

'What about the rest of the campaign?' asked Eitan.

'Three hundred twelve dead,'

'God forgive us,' said Eitan.

'Five hundred fifty-three wounded.'

'That number,' said Alon, 'will increase dramatically once the Syrian operation is concluded.'

'Yes,' said Eitan, 'as to the Syrian situation…'

'We have achieved complete victory there,' said Nagid.

'It does look that way,' said Ben Zvi.

'What orders?'

Eitan did not hesitate. 'Finish your operations there and leave.'

'Of course, Prime Minister.'

'I want to see news reports of our forces withdrawing from the Damascus region by this evening.'

'You shall,' said Nagid.

Alon asked, 'What of surviving Hezbollah forces in Lebanon?'

'Concentrating in the north,' said Nagid.

'What do you propose to do about them?' Alon asked.

'My forces are punishing them with air and artillery strikes.' Nagid cleared his throat. 'Prime Minister, if I may, Christian and Druze militias are mobilized in the Lebanon Mountains.'

'And?'

'If we were to get out the way...'

Eitan laughed. 'You want to unleash them on Hezbollah?'

'Yes.'

Without hesitating Eitan said. 'Very well. But, you are to aid them in no way whatsoever, is that clear?'

'Completely.'

'Prime Minister,' interjected General Ben Zvi, 'I will have a written order to that effect drafted within the hour.'

'Good, General,' said Eitan. 'General Nagid, you will receive that order in the presence of the Security Cabinet and sign it.'

Nagid nodded, 'Of course. Prime Minister?'

'Yes?'

'When we are through here, might I have a word with you in private?'

'What about?'

'I'd like to talk to you about my post military career...'

RIYADH

Prince Abdullah could not stop laughing. 'Look at all the trouble this little girl has caused.'

'Cousin, I hardly think this is the time.'

'Just look, Rafah.'

'I have not had time.'

'The American President's daughter interviewed a pair of Israelis on her television show.' He pointed to the television screen.

'She is pretty,' said Rafah.

'Yes, quite. And now the Lebanese, the Syrians and his opposition at home are screaming that he's in the pocket of the Jews. This is very interesting politics.'

'Yes, but the siege...'

'Yes?'

'Change the channel to al-Jazera, Cousin.'

The prince did so. It showed an image of the palace siege. Even from a distance Abdullah could see what appeared to be several dozen bodies lying in blood before the palace gate. The anchor spoke of growing outrage in the Muslim world.

General Rafah said, 'My men made it seem as if the king's guards did this....'

WASHINGTON DC

'Mr. President,' began Franks, 'Your daughter's interview with the Israeli PR team has caused many problems in the last 24 hours.'

'If I may, Mr. President,' interjected Ambassador Silber, who was on conference call from Jerusalem, 'She's a big hit over here. The networks keep broadcasting the interview.'

'I think it's rather sweet,' said Benard.

'Maybe so,' said Franks, 'But they're raising hell about this over in the Middle East.' Franks grabbed the morning paper and flipped to the editorial section. 'And there is *this*.'

He threw the paper down on the coffee table. 'President Biased for Israel', read the headline, by Arthur Wesson.

'Have you read the piece? Those are some pretty strong claims, sir,' said Franks.

'I have.'

Boddicker spoke, 'Wesson must be marginalized and destroyed.'

'Is that really appropriate?' Davis asked.

'Absolutely,' Boddicker replied.

'I wouldn't put it that way, sir.' said Franks. 'But he's right.'

'I'll start the leaks this afternoon,' said Boddicker. 'I have some blogger friends who will love what I can dish to them.'

Stettler nodded. 'On to more pressing matters, Secretary Davis?'

'The Iranians continue to move forces toward the Straits of Hormuz. These include surface groups and air assets. Lots of mine layers. Iran's three *Kilo* class submarines have left port.'

'What are we doing?' Stettler asked.

Davis took out a piece of paper. 'Our Gulf Task-Force is assembling, sir. Two carrier battle groups, two Marine Expeditionary Units. I also want your permission to mobilize the 82nd Airborne.'

'Jesus,' said Benard.

'Your plan?' asked Stettler.

'We will seize Bandar Abass, Qushm and the surrounding islands.'

'You want to seize Iranian territory?' asked Benard.

'In order to guarantee the straits are open, we will have to.'

'Go on,' said Stettler.

'From there we can conduct operations against Iranian anti-shipping assets deeper into the Gulf.'

'Might we have to go deeper into Iran?' Stettler asked.

'I can't say we won't.'

'Your leading us to a repeat of the Iraq war,' said Benard. 'Is that what we want?'

'We may not have a choice,' said Davis.

Boddicker spoke, 'We should begin consultations with the British.'

'And the French,' said Davis.

'I better get a speech prepared,' said Franks. 'Soon, you may have to go before Congress.'

LEBANON MOUNTAINS

Beta held a bandana up to his nose against the stink. The ditch he stood before was filled with the bodies of Hezbollah fighters. They had fought, save for a handful of young prisoners, down to the last man. The prisoners, hands and feet bound in plastic cuffs, were set in row and leaned up against an APC. While seven of the men simply hung their heads or stared blankly ahead, one of them, he could be no older than 18, Beta thought, could not stop himself from crying.

One of Beta's men asked, 'Can we gag him?'

'I don't think so,' Beta said.

The paratrooper walked up to the crying youth and shouted at him to shut up. Then he kicked the kid in the shins. Beta trotted over and pushed the paratrooper away from the prisoner.

'Go,' Beta said.

The paratrooper walked away mumbling in disgust at the young Hezbollah fighter.

The kid sniffled a bit and said in Arabic. 'Do not kick me.'

'I won't,' said Beta.

'I can help you,' the kid said.

'Really?' replied Beta.

'Yes.'

'How so?'

'My name is Yasser,' he said. 'And I know something you might like to know.'

'Yeah? What is that?'

'The man I used to work for....'

RIYADH

'Would you like to enter the palace?' General Rafah asked.

'No, not yet, Cousin. I should like do so with some suitable pageantry.'

'Upon a white horse?'

'Exactly.'

'Tomorrow then?'

'Yes.'

'I shall make the arrangements.'

'Good,' said Abdullah. 'Where is the former king?'

'Under guard at the airport.'

'Has he said where he would like to go?'

'The king of Morocco has offered to take him.'

'Good.'

'The former king wants assurances that his accounts will not be tampered with.'

'I make no promises.' He paused a moment. 'Is the former king's harem with him?'

General Rafah sighed and rolled his eyes. 'There are other matters to attend to, Cousin.'

'Of course. Send an army brigade to the northeast, and begin transferring a few squadrons there.'

'Yes, Cousin.'

'I want a big show. Make sure there is plenty of press.'

'Al-Jazera?'

'Yes. Also BBC, CNN…'

'It shall be done.'

'Good. And make sure the Israelis know. I want their government fully informed.'

'I shall contact Mossad.'

'What of the Iranians?'

'They continue to mobilize. Most of their naval assets are concentrated in and around Bandar Abbas.'

'And the Americans?'

'Assembling forces as well.'

'How soon do you think they will move?'

'We do not have much time.'

'I will not let the Iranians close the straits.'

JERUSALEM

Sedor waited in his office as the prime minister, back in the official residence, consulted the American president. He didn't worry, there was no point in worrying. He only hoped the Prime Minister wouldn't give away all they gained.

A TV was on in the corner. It was tuned to the BBC. In London the anchor interviewed a pair of retired British generals who appraised the military situation on the ground. Sedor smiled at what they said.

'It is perfectly clear at this point Martin,' said a retired Royal Marine general, 'That the Israelis have won a tremendous victory on the ground, not only against Hezbollah, but Syria as well.'

The anchor turned to the retired army general. 'General St. Claire, would you agree?'

'Absolutely,' he concurred. 'I am particularly impressed with the magnitude of their victory in Lebanon.'

'How so?' asked the anchor.

'In the south and center of the country, it appears Hezbollah has been utterly defeated. Rocket and missile attacks are heavily reduced. Nothing has hit Haifa or Jerusalem in 24 hours.'

'But what about the international crisis? What about world anger against the Israelis. There is talk that Saudi forces are mobilizing in the northwest of the country.'

General St. Claire said, 'I am a military man. This brewing international crisis in a job for the foreign ministry people, I would think.'

It is, Sedor said to himself.

He was interrupted by an aide who handed him a manila folder. 'I don't believe this report,' said the aide, 'But I thought you should see it regardless.'

He nodded, opened it, and read.

'Now this is damn interesting,' Sedor said.

'Do you believe it?' the aide asked. 'I mean, why would a pool boy be fighting in the field?'

'They could be desperate,' Sedor said. 'He's young. Probably didn't want to sit out the fighting.'

'I suppose,' said the aide.

'Think about it,' said Sedor. 'We know this Hornet was somewhere in the north.'

'I suppose this confirms that. So you think this is actionable?'

'I think it is worth an action, yes,' Sedor replied. 'Send this report on to Nagid. Immediately. Tell him I think it's real, and he should act on it right away.'

WASHINGTON DC

Via video monitor from Jerusalem, Ambassador Silber updated the resident. 'The Israelis are withdrawing from Syria.'

'Just withdrawing?' Ambassador Benard asked. 'No preconditions?'

'None,' replied Silber. 'They are heading back to the Golan.'

'Well that's something,' Benard said.

'Now,' said Silber, 'As to Lebanon. Prime Minister Eitan says they will begin withdrawing ground forces in central Lebanon to the Litani within forty-eight hours.'

'What about the Beqaa?' Benard asked.

'She didn't say. When I pressed she said there are no changes planned there.'

'And Beirut?' asked Benard.

'Prime Minister Eitan says they will remain there for up to seven days before withdrawing.'

'Probably want to ransack the city for all the intelligence they can get,' offered Boddicker.

'So at least things are beginning to wind down over there, yes?' asked Stettler.

'Uh…no not really,' said Davis.

'What do you mean, not really?' asked the president.

'There is significant movement now, in Saudi Arabia,' said Boddicker.

'Against the Israelis?' Stettler asked?

'Well, they are moving some assets to the north, but there is massive activity in the east.'

'Activity?' asked Benard.

'Yes, ships heading out of port, aircraft moving toward bases in the gulf.'

'Those moves toward the northwest have been very public,' said Benard. 'I saw a news report about it this morning.'

'But they haven't been talking about these moves toward the Gulf,' said Stettler.

Franks shook his head.

'So what's their game?' the president asked.

'I'd hate to sound optimistic,' said Davis, 'but these deployments look like they're aimed at the Iranians.'

'There's no reason why the Saudis would want the straits to be closed,' said Boddicker.

'Think of the politics of it,' said Franks. 'They make a big deal about sending small forces against Israel.' He looked at Davis, 'It's a small force, right?'

'A few brigades and fighter squadrons,' said the secretary of defense.

'I'm no strategist, but that doesn't seem like very much force against the Israelis,' said Franks.

Davis shook his head. 'Not nearly enough.'

'So,' said Franks, 'They make a big show of this deployment against the Israelis; it distracts their own people.'

'Not to mention the entire region,' said Boddicker.

'Meanwhile, they move to protect their own interests in the Gulf.'

'And remember something else,' said Boddicker, 'A big fear in the Arab world is a return of Persian domination.'

'Prince Abdullah is playing a very strong hand,' said Franks. 'Well done.'

'Alright,' said Stettler. 'I'd like to find out what exactly the Saudis have in mind. Ambassador Benard, would you please summon the Saudi Ambassador to the White House.'

'Yes, Mr. President,' said Benard.

'And have our embassy inform Prince Abdullah that I would like to speak with him at his convenience.'

NORTH BEIRUT

The situation in Lebanon could not have been worse, the Hornet knew.

'At least the Jews are withdrawing from central Lebanon,' said his aide.

'You fool. They are withdrawing because they have accomplished everything they set out to do.'

The large Hezbollah force pinned against the Lebanon Mountains had been annihilated. Resistance in Beirut had crumbled. Hezbollah's rocket forces were all but neutralized. The war was going so badly that even the nation's Druze leadership, whose people's survival had always depended upon choosing the winning side, was delivering fiery speeches against Hezbollah.

'What is the disposition of Druze forces?'

'Gathering within their enclaves east of Beirut,' said Ali.

'And our forces?'

'We have nearly 2,000 fighters in the north. They are now concentrating along the Syrian border. Lebanese army troops have already stopped the entry of our fighters into Tripoli.'

'We cannot expect any help from the Syrians,' said the Hornet. 'Any units in the south or center of the country?'

'Small pockets of fighters, only. We are not in contact with them…'

The Hornet heard the rotor blades but thought nothing of it. After all, the sky had been filled with aircraft for days. Not until the table he was sitting at began to vibrate did he realize what was happening. Ali ran to the window and pulled open the curtain. He turned to speak, but before he could say anything the wall disintegrated in a hail of bullets…

JERUSALEM

'Prime Minister,' said Sedor, 'We got him.'

'Are you sure?'

'Yes. The villa had a mountain of intelligence, maps and documents. The senior field commanders we have captured confirm the target's existence, though they have never met him. We are waiting for our intelligence source, the captured boy, to confirm a death photo. But it's him.'

Nobody spoke for a few moments. 'Have we won?' asked Eitan.

General Ben Zvi spoke. 'Prime Minister, we have done everything we set out to do. We have severely damaged Iran's nuclear program. We have battered Hezbollah beyond recognition. What's left right now is being attacked by the Druze militia. Christian forces there are threatening to intervene as well.'

'What about Syria?' she asked.

'Our forces are back on the Golan. Syrian forces are falling back around Damascus.'

'Alright, good,' said Eitan. 'I want to expedite our withdraw from Lebanon. Get our forces out of the Beqaa as soon as possible.'

'Yes, Prime Minister,' said Ben Zvi.

'And speed up our pullback from Beirut.'

'Yes, Prime Minister. There are reports of Syrian troops infiltrating into northern Lebanon. May I take action against them?'

'Yes,' said the prime minister. 'Aerial only.'

'We can interdict them from the air. But we can't stop them.'

'Do the best you can.'

'Also, contact the Americans. Offer to hand over control of Beirut Airport to them.'

'To help with relief operations?' asked Ben Zvi.

'Yes. It will look good. And organize army relief supplies as well. I want large stacks of food stuffs with our flag on them. Make sure the international press sees.'

'Yes, Prime Minister.'

'Organize efforts for the Palestinian refugee camps in Lebanon as well.'

'A wise move, if you don't mind my saying,' said Ben Zvi.

'This is all well and good, but what of the Iranians?' asked Shoal.

'Everything they are doing seems to be directed at the Straits of Hormuz and not us.'

'That is a problem for the Americans,' said Eitan.

WASHINGTON DC

President Stettler spoke, 'Prince Abdullah, before we begin, by what title shall I address you?'

'Mr. President,' said the Prince in perfect English, 'Prince Abdullah will suffice for now.'

'Very well.'

'Mr. President, I would like to thank you for your interest in the region,' said the prince in a tone which sounded very accommodating and deferential, 'The Middle East is a far more stable place when America is involved.'

'I appreciate that, Prince. And I am grateful for your taking this time to consult with me.'

'Not at all, Mr. President. I hope to foster stronger relations with the United States than our two countries have enjoyed in the past decade.'

'As do I,' replied Stettler.

'Now. Mr. President, may I ask you a blunt question?'

'Please.'

'What is your stance toward my country and our new government?'

'I think that is a fair question, Prince Abdullah.' Stettler paused for a moment and collected his thoughts, 'The United States views recent events there as the internal affairs of your kingdom.'

'I am most gratified to hear you say that, Mr. President.'

'We would, though be most happy if we saw your government in the coming years become more...shall we say, modern.'

'Mr. President, my country must make many changes if we are to thrive in the 21st century. Those changes will, of course, take time and have to be gradual.'

'Of course. How can we help?'

'I think, Mr. President, the United States can help, but not before the new government is established, ' said Prince Abdullah. 'Also, the current situation in the Middle East does not lend itself easily to reform.'

'I agree completely.'

'May I ask another tough question of you, Mr. President?'

'Yes.'

'Do you intend to let the Israelis continue making war on Syria and Lebanon?'

'Prince Abdullah, Israel does not take action on my orders. But I would like to inform you that Prime Minister Eitan has assured me her nation is beginning the process of withdrawal from Lebanon. As you know, they are already pulling back from Syria.'

'Yes, I know. I do hope the Israelis will leave Lebanon in peace.'

'As do I, Prince Abdullah.'

'I would like, now, Mr. President to discuss matters in the Persian Gulf.'

'I would as well.'

'Mr. President, I must ask you to keep your navy out of the gulf region.'

'We have taken no action, yet, Prince Abdullah,' said Stettler.

'Mr. President, we know you have assembled a large task-force in the Indian Ocean, including your Marines.'

'We have. We are very concerned about Iranian action in the Straits of Hormuz.'

'We too are aware of these actions. But I must warn you, Mr. President, that if America attacks a Muslim country, that would be a catastrophe for the region.'

'We must guarantee free navigation of the straits.'

'That is in my country's interest as well, Mr. President. And we will act accordingly.'

'How so, if I may ask?'

'My navy and air force are positioned to keep the straits open.'

'What will you do?'

'We will not allow the straits to be closed, Mr. President, and we will use force to keep them open...'

JERUSALEM

Prime Minister Eitan sat behind her desk. Before her were Generals Ben Zvi, Nagid and Peled.

'You are all to be congratulated,' began the prime minister.

'Congratulate my pilots, Prime Minister,' said Peled.

'I will, General, in due time.'

'I would like that, Prime Minister.'

'In a few days the four of us will convene a press conference. You two,' she pointed to Nagid and Peled, 'will walk the press through your campaigns.'

Peled nodded reluctantly. Nagid could not contain his smile.

'Now, to business,' the prime minister said. 'Have we won?'

Peled furrowed his brow. 'Forgive me, Prime Minister, but I do not like to make such bold statements.'

'I must insist.'

Peled rubbed his chin. 'The Iranian weapons program has been crippled....retaliation by Iran was prevented because we devastated their command and control...'

Nagid added, 'Do not forget the Syrian air force.'

'Yes of course,' said Peled. 'Well, we didn't lose.'

'Come General Peled,' said Nagid, 'You are being too modest. You have waged the greatest aerial campaign in history. You are the Ariel Sharon of the Israeli Air Force. No, that is not going far enough. You are its Caesar!'

'That is not for me to say, General Nagid.'

Eitan spoke, 'Now, General Nagid, what is your assessment?'

'All that is left for me to do is write my memoirs.' He laughed. 'I think the word *victory* will be in the title.'

WASHINGTON DC

'Daddy, I'm sorry I made so much trouble for you on my show.'

'Kelly, you didn't make any trouble.'

'But what they said about you--'

Stettler held out a hand, 'To hell with them.'

'Why do you think they don't like Israel?'

Stettler shook his head. 'I don't know, sweetie. It would take me too long to explain.'

'I want to know.'

Kelly's phone buzzed.

'You better get that,' he said.

She nodded nonchalantly to her phone, 'I'll let it buzz. Where did it all start?'

Stettler laughed, 'Well, you see, in the beginning...'

PART IV
EPILOGUE

How to know you have defeated a non-state actor

-Victory is not widely doubted at home

-Troops return home proud of their service

-The non-state actor's surviving leadership remains underground.

-Proxies for the non-state actor complain of war crimes

-Proxies for the non-state actor invent metrics to prove the non-state actor won

-Proxies use law-fare against your civilian and military leadership

-Your own leadership calls an early election

Digital Victory in Modern War
Professor Annon Statch

Let there be no doubt, Saudi Arabia will be an Islamic country, dedicated to Mohamed, PBUH, and his teachings. The Koran will be our grand book, a source for our law. But it will not be the only law. For too long, those dedicated to the Holy Koran have thought only of that great book. But there are other great books, steeped in the knowledge of humanity. That knowledge is sacred. Did not science lead to the wonderful inventions of radio, television and the Internet? Do we, the believers of Mohamed, PBUH, not use these inventions to spread his word? Would the so called faithful leave Islam consigned to a few deserts in the backwaters of the globe?

The so-called true believers say science is the religion of the unfaithful. I say, let them be unfaithful. If they cannot comprehend the words and deeds of science, let them not comprehend. They will answer to Mohamed, PBUH.

The New Arabia, Abdullah al - Saud,
Prince Regent of Arabia

Many in the so-called Peace Party say the price of our victory in Lebanon was too high. I ask them, what would be the price of defeat? Would they pay that?

Not Peace, but Victory, by General Natan Nagid:
The Man who Would Lead Israel

WASHINGTON DC

'Good evening folks. I'm here tonight with Rafael Gould, the Israeli journalist whose book, *Gonzo War*, is number one on the New York Times best seller list. Thank you for joining us, Rafael.'

'It's my pleasure to be here, Bill.'

'Now, in addition to your own book, you also helped General Natan Nagid write his popular, and I might add, controversial memoir of the war.'

'Well, Bill, I wouldn't say I helped. I organized his notes. He and I discussed the craft of writing, but I really didn't help. I don't think he really needs help with anything.'

'Well put, Rafael. Do you think General Nagid would make a good PM?'

Gonzo smiled sheepishly and laughed.

JERUSALEM

'We see Prime Minister Eitan now, making her way toward the dais, no doubt elated with the election news that her party, which had merged with two smaller parties, has secured, on its own, an absolute majority in the Knesset...She is at the podium now...and there we see her close confidant, likely minister of defence, and newest member of the Knesset, Natan Nagid...He is all smiles, isn't he?'

CINCINNATI

'President Stettler, as you know, polls are extremely tight, and with the election just eleven days away, political scientists say the race between you and the senator from Colorado is a tossup. With the nation seeing strong economic growth this year, many feel the race will come down to foreign policy. The senator has been very critical of your handling of the Middle East Crisis. Would you care to respond?'

'Yes I would, thank you Jim. First, if I could say one thing on the economy, yes, we've come a long way, we are doing well, but I'm not satisfied yet. We can be doing even better. Now, as to the Middle East Crisis why don't we take a look at the record. I had a lot of good people working for me, Director Boddicker, Ambassador Benard, Secretary

Davis, and I think the first, and most important result of our effort is this; we kept the United States out of the war. And let me tell you, Jim, let me tell America, there was a night when I went to bed thinking I was going to have to order an attack on Iran. But thanks to my administration's hard work, that wasn't necessary. Now, let's take a look at the Middle East.

'Lord knows it could be better. Syria is right now a closed off, paranoid basket case. Lebanon sadly has descended into a three-way civil war. But the region could be much worse. The Saudi Prince Regent is determined to modernize his country. The nuclear weapons program in Iran has been badly hobbled and it will be many years before the Iranians can assemble a nuclear weapon. More importantly, Iran is seeing massive democracy protests, which my administration encourages and supports. Just last week I met with a delegation of Iranian dissidents and exiles. And if I may Jim, my daughter interviewed a pair of brave, young activists on MTV. And in case you're wondering fellas, she's still available...'

WILLIAM STROOCK

A LINE THROUGH THE DESERT

ALWAYS READY! SECOND TO NONE!

Jake Bloom doesn't like high school very much and he's always felt out of place in his synagogue. He's not thrilled with his parents either. But he loves Led Zeppelin and his girlfriend, Patricia. Seeking to emulate the Israeli soldiers he's always admired, much to the horror of his over protective parents, Jake joins the army the day after graduation high school. When his summer romance with Patricia ends in heartbreak, as it must, Jake leaves for the army jaded and embittered. In the elite 2nd Armored Cavalry Regiment Jake finds the purpose and brotherhood he's always yearned for. When the regiment is deployed to the Persian Gulf as part of Operation Desert Storm Jake meets the challenges of tedium, duty, and the horrors of war with honor and good humor – who knew you could blast heavy metal music at the Iraqis? Now if he could only put Patricia out of his mind...

"Pitch perfect." *Omri Ceren, Mere Rhetoric*

"Stroock has done a good job of capturing the life of a soldier in a combat unit throughout his service in Germany and the Middle East." *General Phil Bolte, Cavalry Journal*

"Stroock not only tells us about military life, he makes us feel it." *William Katz, Urgent Agenda*

"Jewish 'Jarhead'....with the GenX *attitude* **Stroock brings to this unsentimental, fast-paced book, should make it a favorite with history and military buffs."** *Kathy Shaidle, Examiner.com*

"I found myself thoroughly enjoying To Defend the Earth. It's part military history, part sci-fi short story collection that takes a believable approach to a scenario as fantastic as Alien Invasion and gives us a glimpse into a cross section of people dealing with a world in tatters." - Steve McLauchlan, WWPD.net.

"The book is fast-paced, even with some lengthy, detailed battle sequences, no doubt reflecting Stroock's interest in military history. But what I really liked about it is how Stroock did something different with this well-worn genre, instead of going the cliched route." Aussie Dave, Israellycool.com

"This is far from the B- grade story your wallet fears wasting money on. So ask your library for it or go to Amazon and buy, as I did. You won't regret it!" Battleblue1.com

"Overall this book is well worth the 99 cents being charged, if you own a e-reader or a kindle and your looking for a quick fun read, this book is for you." Ml40k.com